June 12, 2012

TASTE OF FIRE

About the Author:
Jeannie Faulkner Barber was born and raised in Marshall, Texas. Writing has been one of two passions in her life, the other being drag racing: she drives her own race car. She met her husband Monte at the track. She is an active member of the East Texas Writers Association. She currently lives in Kilgore, Texas with Monte. They have three sons and nine grandchildren.

Other Books by Jeannie Faulkner Barber:
Scent of Double Deception (with Ann Alan)

TASTE OF FIRE

JEANNIE FAULKNER BARBER

DESERT COYOTE PRODUCTIONS
SCOTTS VALLEY, CALIFORNIA

Text other than quoted material © 2012 Jeannie Faulkner Barber.
Cover design © 2012 Stacey Martinez.
All rights reserved.

No part of this publication may be reproduced, stored in a retrieval system, or transmitted in any form or by any means, electronic, mechanical, photocopying, recording, or otherwise without the express written consent of the author.

This is a work of fiction. Any resemblance to real events or persons, living or dead, is coincidental.

Library of Congress Control Number: 2012936021
EAN-13: 978-1-475-08377-4
ISBN-10: 1-475-08377-7

Typeset in 11pt Book Antiqua
Printed in the U.S.A.
First edition 2012

To my Lord and Savior who gave me insight, talent, creativity, resourcefulness, stubbornness, and an open door to follow the journey through this chapter of my life.

ॐ ೲೲ ॐ

Taste of Fire *is dedicated to all firefighters, men or women, young or old, active or veteran, paid or volunteer, whose artful and noble heroism I applaud. May God always guide every step to keep you safe.*

Acknowledgments

To my wonderful and devoted husband, Monte Barber, thank you for being my rock and biggest fan. You're my Crew Chief and best critic. I love you more every day.

Our sons, Joe Bryan Barber, Adam Clay, Garry Clay, and my nephew, Randy Summers, and their families … a grateful thank you for belief and encouragement to grab the brass ring toward my writing goals.

My sister, Faye Summers, who I affectionately call 'Punk', read to me, invented the 'Wooly Worms', and gave my imagination a jump-start as a little girl. I will cherish those memories forever. You always colored my world.

Bernadette Thompson Martin and her creative husband Ken, who championed my efforts and talent across the miles … it was *destined* for us to become friends!

Don A. Martinez, Editor and Publisher of Desert Coyote Productions, and his wife, Stacey—thanks for acceptance, instruction, guidance, and direction, which completed the circle to make my dreams a reality.

Thank you, J.R. Rodgers for providing the truisms of what a real volunteer firefighter encounters and uses. Your youthfulness brought a heightened insight to my writing.

My artistic friend, Joe M. Jones, selflessly supplied time and talent to advance my efforts. Your Texas Press Association award winning photos enhanced the book and trailer, which visually imparted the treacherous veracity all firefighters experience.

In addition, new friends, Kim and Curtis Riley, thank you for being so dedicated. Without your help and diligence, I would not have obtained those intense firefighting pictures Leigh Merritt shot. The fact is sometimes heroes live right next door.

I will always be grateful to my writing groups and fellow 'critters' in our critique group. Keep writing!

Nicholas Shaw — Mr. Personality, a hug of thanks for utilizing your ingenious resourcefulness to promote and sell my books. You are a treasured jewel of a friend.

A Special Recognition

To me, 2011 was "The Year of Texas Blazes." Our drought-ridden territory suffered scorching temperatures of 100-plus degrees for months. The parched land only served as a catalyst to stoke the savage fury of wildfires. Texas spans more than 170 million acres, and no section of my enormous home State was exempt from the treacherous wrath.

Helpless, I watched the leaves of even young saplings turn an out-of-season brown from lack of rain. Huge oaks, elms, and varieties of evergreen pines lost footing. Too often, their struggling root systems surrendered. Statuesque timbers tumbled with the implosion of an outdated condemned building. At times, high lines became victims in the wake to spark yet another horrific fire.

I felt as if the uncontrollable devastation, not to mention fear, held my feet and heart in concrete. Folders with birth certificates, college transcripts, precious pictures, childhood memorabilia from our sons and grandkids, along with my Bible filled the trunk of my car. I tried to stay calm, but prepared for a speedy retreat.

Firefighters, either paid employees or volunteers, valiantly emerged with the courage of a dragon slayer to extinguish the enemy again and again. Men and women, young and mature, launched into practiced action every time the call went out to save land, homes, and lives. Each one is a modern day hero.

Therefore, I want to personally praise all the brave "catastrophe warriors" and recognize their gallant and selfless acts through my mystery novel, *Taste of Fire*.

Thank you … thank you … and God bless you!

The following are quotes from various fire department personnel I spoke to regarding the 2011 wildfire circumstances:

"The severity of the constant situation made the fear visible in the eyes of each one of my firefighters." **–Joe Johnston, Fire Chief, Sabine Volunteer Fire Department, Liberty City Community, Kilgore, Texas**

"We have approximately twenty-seven on staff. Most of all, our department could not have functioned, or continue to function now, without the help and contributions from the good citizens we serve." **–Bill Wall, Fire Chief, Overton Fire Department, Overton, Texas**

"I'm so thankful to the people who gave their time and energy to support us. The communities truly rallied to help our efforts. It made me so proud." **–John Hendon (73 years young), New London Fire Department, New London, Texas**

"We say, 'put the wet stuff on the red stuff.' The worst came Labor Day weekend, 2011. The whole next week, I missed school to help keep our communities from burning up. The State provided a letter to excuse my absences. I knew where I needed to be, and that particular week it was fighting fires." **–J.R. Rodgers (15 years old), New London Fire Department, New London, Texas**

"The worst thing as a firefighter is to have to tell a family to evacuate their home. We even had one fireman whose house was evacuated while he was working the fires. I'm proud to say, we did not lose a single home. It could not have been accomplished without the help and support of our communities pulling together, as well as neighboring fire departments. Many of us took our vacation and sick leave to be available to fight the fires. Regardless, it isn't a sacrifice to us. It's our calling." **–Curtis Riley, Fire Chief, New London Fire Department, New London, Texas. Mr. Riley's grandfather, S.M. Riley, was a charter**

member, and Curtis is a 3rd generation firefighter with the New London Fire Department.

Table of Contents

PROLOGUE 1
CHAPTER ONE 3
CHAPTER TWO 8
CHAPTER THREE 12
CHAPTER FOUR 18
CHAPTER FIVE 22
CHAPTER SIX... 28
CHAPTER SEVEN 36
CHAPTER EIGHT 40
CHAPTER NINE 51
CHAPTER TEN 57
CHAPTER ELEVEN 62
CHAPTER TWELVE 67
CHAPTER THIRTEEN 74
CHAPTER FOURTEEN 79
CHAPTER FIFTEEN... 83
CHAPTER SIXTEEN 86
CHAPTER SEVENTEEN 92
CHAPTER EIGHTEEN 97
CHAPTER NINETEEN 103
CHAPTER TWENTY... 111
CHAPTER TWENTY ONE 116
CHAPTER TWENTY TWO 122
CHAPTER TWENTY THREE 126
CHAPTER TWENTY FOUR 131
CHAPTER TWENTY FIVE 139
CHAPTER TWENTY SIX 146

CHAPTER TWENTY SEVEN......................... 154
CHAPTER TWENTY EIGHT 158
CHAPTER TWENTY NINE 164
CHAPTER THIRTY.. 171
CHAPTER THIRTY ONE................................ 180
CHAPTER THIRTY TWO 186
CHAPTER THIRTY THREE 194
CHAPTER THIRTY FOUR 198
CHAPTER THIRTY FIVE 202
CHAPTER THIRTY SIX................................... 211
CHAPTER THIRTY SEVEN 218
CHAPTER THIRTY EIGHT 224

Taste of Fire

PROLOGUE

May 18, 1985

Goosebumps marched over the young woman's skin as she reached across the dining room table for her purse. A pink and white Sippy cup toppled in the wake of her anxiety. Reflexes sluggish, she tried to rescue the plastic container full of milk, but it cracked against the hardwood floor. White liquid splattered like a strand of broken pearls.

"Damn it." With the tang of alcohol on her tongue, the words slurred.

A denim work shirt on a nearby chair substituted for a paper towel, but it only smeared the mess. "Sweet Jesus, I don't need this right now."

Damp shirt tossed aside, she scooped up the little girl out of the playpen.

A ragged, teddy bear fell from the child's chubby hand. "Bawh, bawh."

"Oh sweetheart, you don't need it."

A tiny bottom lip protruded and wails for the bear began.

The woman scrambled to retrieve the wayward toy. "Okay, okay honey. Please don't cry."

In the kitchen, the refrigerator door swung open, and streaks of light danced on the dark wall. Baby bottle in one hand, car keys in the other, she repositioned the toddler on her hip. "We have to go. I hope to God I can get out of here before …"

"Before what?" a deep male voice blared from the hallway.

The wooden frame banged shut as she ran out the back door.

"Stop!" he growled.

TASTE OF FIRE

Unnerved, she scooted the small child inside the car. In one quick move, she jammed the key into the ignition and hit the lock button.

A mountain of a man appeared at the driver's side window just as the doors clicked shut. Vile curses flew. "Open the damn door." A meaty fist crushed down on the hood. "Now!"

Thunder rumbled in a starless sky, and mammoth raindrops pelted the windshield.

Terrified, she jerked the car into gear to escape.

CHAPTER ONE

Present Year

A lightshow of red and blue flashes pierced the ebony night in Anniston, Alabama like Roman candles on the Fourth of July. The speeding ambulance zigzagged from lane to lane while the siren screamed for attention.

Terri Neal glanced out one of the small back windows. A sea of traffic parted on the Interstate. Headlights, from cars yielded on the side of the road, took on the appearance of fuzzy owl eyes. A hideous odor of burnt flesh permeated the vehicle. The unpredictable sway of the emergency route caused the IV to slap against her arm. She looked down at a young girl whose eyelids flickered.

Face ashen white, the victim gasped for breath and strained to raise a hand.

"Hang on. We're almost to the hospital. I won't leave you—fight, fight to live." *I'm not even supposed to go in the ambulance, I'm a firefighter, but dear Lord this girl cannot give up ... not now ... not on my watch.*

Terri rode shotgun in Engine Number Five, the first to arrive on the scene. A shiver prickled across her shoulders at the horrific sight.

An unimaginable mass of twisted, tangled metal blocked the road. Reflective shards of glass littered the thoroughfare like luminescent confetti. Steam boiled from a wrecked vehicle, and a mixture of fluids gushed onto the asphalt.

Traffic halted, and onlookers began to gather around.

In a violent flash, the compact car's gas tank exploded, and the scene turned into a sadistic inferno.

TASTE OF FIRE

Flames spewed like spherical daggers as if to dare anyone to approach, and the profound illumination was blinding.

Above the crackle and hiss, a female voice screamed for help.

The crew from Station House Six jumped into precision action preparing a legion of heavy snake-like hoses to propel water on the obvious tragedy.

After a diligent twelve-hour shift, pure adrenaline fueled Terri's senses. *Oh God – car fires.* Halligan bar in hand, she rushed toward the calamitous debris, worked feverishly to wrestle open the door, and freed the driver.

Persistent plumes of choking, black smoke billowed upward, haloed by the glare of holocaustic fire.

Two other firefighters took over after Terri fell to the ground, throat raw from toxic fumes.

Soon, paramedics snapped open a gurney and secured the victim, ready to transport. "We've got it from here, but are you okay?" One of the rescue workers squatted beside Terri.

She shrugged off the heavy turnout jacket. "Yeah, Jeff, I'm fine."

"Please. Go with me. I want her to go, too," the girl hoarsely begged.

After a slight nod, Terri climbed inside the ambulance and slipped off the rest of the protective gear. "Uh, can you tell me your name? What happened?"

"Celia, Celia Wisner. Just left night class at the … the community college." The girl coughed hard. "Guess a tire blew. My car flipped over and over. Oh God, don't let me die!" Tears streaked her cheeks. "My parents …"

4

"Shhh, don't talk any more. Save your strength." Terri took her hand.

The ambulance screeched to a halt in the portico of the Griffin County Hospital. Emergency room doors flew open, and paramedics rushed the girl inside to prepared hospital staff.

"Hang in there, Celia. I'll wait right here." The words trailed as the group disappeared down a long corridor.

In the sterile dull environment, Terri dropped down on one of the black vinyl chairs in the waiting room. The frigid temperature eased frayed nerves. She grabbed a nearby box of tissue to wipe soot and sweat from her face. *I have to know the outcome. I can't leave – I gave my word.*

Two seats over, a Hispanic woman stared at the cover of a tattered magazine. Across the room, an older black couple huddled close, each crying softly. The constant tick of a large numbered clock on the wall added to the angst-filled milieu.

Arms crossed, Terri tried to focus on the blue linoleum squares of the shiny buffed floor to pass the time. Before long, exhaustion overtook, vision dimmed, and she closed her eyes.

Footsteps echoed in the hallway, and she shot a glance at the big clock. *What? Did I doze off? Over an hour has passed.*

"Ma'am, are you a family member of the car wreck victim?" An unfamiliar voice asked.

She forced herself to stand. "No. I'm Terri Neal, the first firefighter on the scene. Celia is her name. The girl asked me to ride in the ambulance, not to leave her. Are things okay? I mean, did …?" She looked into the navy blue eyes of a man in soiled green scrubs. A doe brown curl lay to one side of his forehead. He extended a hand, and she accepted. His warm hand clutched her clammy one.

"I'm Dr. Abraham, Tucker Abraham. I'm very sorry for your loss. The young woman succumbed to the injuries. We fought hard. She did, too, but smoke inhalation caused the lungs to collapse. There was major damage to several other vital organs, apparent third degree burns, and internal bleeding from the impact."

In Terri's profession, unhappy endings happened often, but tonight touched the core of her soul.

"Ms. Neal, do you think you can notify the next of kin for us?" He continued to cuddle her hand.

"Sure, Dr. Abraham." A long sigh escaped.

"You look tired. Are you okay?"

She recognized sincere compassion, and it gave a thread of inner strength. The calm demeanor made her feel like they were old friends. She pondered his bedside manner. The crooked stethoscope around his neck and stained clothes gave indication of an honest effort.

"Look, please don't be offended. My shift is over in another thirty minutes. Would you like to get some coffee? There's a little café around the corner, or we could have a cup here in the cafeteria."

Coffee? I don't need coffee. I need liquor and lots of it. She released his hand. "I'm not offended at all, but I have to return to the Station. Gotta finish the paperwork. You understand, don't you?"

"Sure, perhaps another time?" The corners of his mouth turned upward.

"How about a rain check?"

"A rain check it is, Firefighter Neal."

She took a couple steps backward. "Listen, thanks for the invitation and whatever you tried to do for, uh, Celia."

"It's my job, but every life is important to me. I feel certain you put forth a valiant attempt as well."

They stood silent for a moment before she turned to walk away. The heavy emergency room doors swished open, and she glanced back.

Dr. Abraham smiled and waved.

CHAPTER TWO

A patina of neon beer signs tinted the counter at the Short Cut Bar & Grill. The smell of grilled onions and peppers wafted through Frank Gunnison's little café.

"Heard on the scanner 'bout the wreck on County Road 58. Sounded like a pretty rough one." He poured a shot of whiskey and handed it to Terri.

Head back, she swallowed the liquor in one gulp. "Rough doesn't come close—try atrocious, Frank. Turned out to be a compact death trap." She pushed the jigger forward. "I need another."

The amber liquid filled the small glass. "Alcohol ain't the answer to conquer those old ghosts, honey."

She chugged it, grabbed a lemon wedge from a wooden bowl, and bit down.

"You never drink over two shots, and I believe you hit that limit about three back. Course, I ain't gonna preach to you."

"Good 'cause I'm not in the mood for a sermon." Hands raised, she stared at the bartender. "The thing is, I can fight a house or building fire all day long, but car fires are … well, different. I've done this for ten years, since I was twenty. It's all I ever wanted to do. So, I can't cringe and be a sissy just because I'm female."

"Don't give me that. You became a firefighter because of your daddy. It was *his* life-long dream, and you chose to assume the role after he died. End of story." Frank paused. "Look, the man did a bang up job to raise you by himself. He didn't have a clue about babies, for sure not little girls. You grew up in the

Station House around rowdy guys who spoiled you rotten."

"I had a good childhood though." A finger twisted a long black curl.

Frank reached for a clean towel from under the counter. "What happened between him and your mama was hard."

"I do *not* want to talk about my mother."

"I didn't mean to bring up any bad memories, I ..."

"Don't go there, and lower your voice. I don't want everyone in here to know my life story for pity's sake."

"Sure thing, sweetheart." He pulled out an antique pocket watch, took the corner of the towel, and rubbed the shiny timepiece. "Life sure gets away, don't it? Uh, I believe you're gonna hit the big 3-0 before long."

"Don't remind me." Terri propped an elbow on the bar.

"All kinds of good things might happen once ya quit thinking you're still a teenybopper." The cloth fell to the counter.

"What? I'll show you a teenybopper." Cloth in hand, she chunked it at him.

He ducked and let out a loud laugh. "Gotta go get some more from the back — seems *somebody* messed up the last clean one."

"You started it, you old geezer."

Frank hobbled to the storage door, unlocked it, and brought back a stack of fresh towels.

"Does your knee hurt tonight? I noticed the limp is a bit more prominent."

"Yup, probably means a change in the weather, but I'm fine."

"Remember when I was five and tried to climb upon your lap, but my heel hit your knee? You yelped like a scared dog, and I asked what was wrong."

"Yeah, and remember the waterfall of tears down your chubby pink cheeks?"

"I didn't cry that much."

"Yes you did and wanted to know how I got my big 'boo boo'. I told you from Viet Nam, and you said ..."

Terri interrupted, "I said, Viet Nam must not be a very nice little boy."

They broke into laughter.

"One more for the road," a gruff voice demanded.

At the end of the counter, a customer sat sideways on the stool, shoulders slumped. A shabby Braves cap shadowed the face. Errant strands of oily brown hair strayed to the edge of a stained collar. The man raised a beer mug in the air. "How 'bout some damn service?" It slammed hard on the wooden counter.

"Okay, okay, don't be so rough on the inventory," Frank replied.

"Inventory? I'm gonna take inventory, all right."

The heavy glass spiraled through the air and shattered on the floor near Terri's feet.

Only music from the jukebox filled the room as silence fell over the bar.

"Get the hell outta my place before I call the cops. I know you don't want *their* company."

The man stood and walked over to Terri. "You're pretty cute, Missy. I think I want *your* company. Why don't me and you spend some quality time together?"

Before she could speak, the click of a gun interrupted.

Taste of Fire

Straight and still, Frank pointed a .357 Magnum at the patron. "Guess you don't hear so good. Maybe I need to clean out your ears. I said **leave**."

"Now Frank, don't be so hard on the guy," Terri said. "I might want to give this big ol' fella something tonight he's never had before." She pursed her lips and leaned forward.

"Yeah, *Frank,* maybe I'm gonna get something tonight I ain't ever …"

In one quick move, she grabbed a handful of his crotch and jerked downward. The man's eyes rolled backward as she planted a foot in the middle of the intruder's chest.

He reeled against an empty table where a half-full pitcher of beer sat. The thick container slid off and crashed in his face. Like an angry volcano, blood erupted from a large gash across his nose.

Frank slid the gun back under the counter and turned to Terri. "Hmm, I believe you're right. I think that might be something he ain't ever had."

Terri dusted off her hands and repositioned on the stool. "Better call 9-1-1."

CHAPTER THREE

"Geeze Louise, did you cause all this mess, Terri Neal?" The paramedic's eyes widened.

She kicked a jagged wedge of glass toward the door. "Hey, the big jerk had it coming."

"Man, what'd he do?"

"First, Frank asked him nice-like to leave, but he launched a beer mug at me. Next, he said he thought me and him oughta spend a little quality time together … so we did."

Paco Taliaferro grinned. "Dang girl, I only transferred in about two months ago." The latex gloves popped as the EMT pulled them on. "I sorta thought I might ask you out some time, but where I come from the girls aren't so mean."

"Oh, I bet there are some bad-ass senoritas in South Texas, too."

"Don't let her fool you Paco, she likes attention, just depends on how you approach the lady." The blond-haired cop placed an arm around Terri's shoulder and gave a little squeeze. "Now am I right, or am I right?" The smile produced perfect white teeth.

"No, the *fool* here is Sergeant Parker Green." Terri glared into his chestnut hazel eyes.

The paramedic shook his head. "I'll take care of the dude on the floor. You two can chatter nonsense all you want, but I'm thinking you missed your calling, woman. Why not apply for the SWAT team next?"

"What're you doing here? This is graveyard shift, Parker. I thought they put you on days, permanent."

"Mason's wife went into labor early. He's the proud daddy of an eight pound little boy. I told the Chief I'd do doubles for the rest of the week." With a foot propped on the rung of the stool, he leaned on the counter. "Frank, you want to press charges tonight?"

A young cop entered, and the sergeant motioned for him to cuff the thug.

"Guess not, but I suppose it's really up to Terri. She's the one he wanted to slobber all over. However, he did bust up one of my best mugs."

Parker yanked the drunk to his feet. "I'll do whatever ya'll want, but it looks like he got the worst end of things. I think she might have even sobered him up a bit."

"Tell ya what, Sarge. If you follow the ambulance to the ER, be sure and give him one of your famous 'straighten up buddy' talks, and we'll call it even." Frank chuckled.

"Either way, he gets a fat fine courtesy of the Anniston Police Department for public intoxication. After a brief checkup at the hospital, I'll be his personal valet. Meanwhile, you two try to stay out of trouble, okay?"

"I'll help the old man behind the counter clean up." Terri slid off the stool. "Oh yeah, and tell Mason congrats for me."

"Will do." The sergeant shoved the man toward the door, and the other officer took over.

Sirens faded, and Frank retrieved a yellow, wheeled bucket full of water from the back room. Sweat beads dotted his brow as he labored to remove the spilt liquor. The heavy mop sloshed and slapped against the laminate wood floor.

Until now, Terri hadn't noticed the dark circles under his eyes or the fact gray filtered throughout his thinning hair. Life for her included work, the Short Cut

Bar and Grill, and Frank—her adopted uncle. He was there when she learned to ride a bike, dressed up for the first prom, graduated high school, and left for college. Frank Gunnison was like a brother to her father, Charles Terrance Neal.

She swept the splintered glass into a tray. The thick slivers clattered against empty cans, bottles, and debris in the trashcan.

After they finished, she sat back down on the barstool.

"Okay, I'd like to get back to our conversation before all the stupid commotion happened." Frank popped the cap off a longneck.

"What conversation? If you mean my mother, I said forget it."

"No honey, the wreck out on 58. Look, I've known you almost since the day you came into this rough, old world. A scrawny, dark brown-eyed tomboy grew into an attractive, intelligent, spunky woman. You took in every stray cat and dog and gave 'em food and love or mended every broken baby bird wing you found. I heard you say over and over how you wanted to be a nurse one day, but your daddy's ideas changed all that."

She smiled as he spoke. *It never occurred to me someone paid attention to those childhood dreams.*

He touched her arm, but she jerked away. "How can you talk about Chuck Neal in such a manner? You were best friends all the way back to junior high. Where's the loyalty? Is the bond gone now that he's dead? Do you believe the rumors, too?" A hand slapped the counter. "Daddy didn't kill himself, Frank. He didn't!"

"No, no sweetheart. All I'm saying is you continue to do things to please everyone, everyone except Terri.

"Oh yeah?"

"Yeah, and I'll tell you what I think you need to do about it." Frank pointed the bottle of beer at her. "Go out on a date, take a trip. Heck, get crazy and have some *real* fun for a change."

"I gotta go."

"Wait. Speaking of change, there's a guy I'd like you to meet, a newcomer who stops by for a sandwich a couple times a week. Seems to be a really nice fella and works over at the ..."

Have some real fun for a change. The comment came back. "You ready to shut this place down?"

"Huh? Sure. I've seen enough excitement for one night. Are you gone?"

Frank mumbled on, but Terri already tuned him out.

♦♦♦♦

The locker door in Station House Six clanked shut. Terri sat down on the long bench and stared straight ahead. The gunmetal cabinets reminded her of soldiers standing at attention. She took a deep breath and closed her eyes. Snippets of flames, screams, sirens, and a handsome doctor's smile whirled. The look in Celia Wisner's tear-filled eyes revealed the obvious; death whispered her name. *Why? Others survive car fires. Why didn't she?*

"How are you, Neal?" a familiar voice interrupted the reverie. "The girl didn't make it, right?"

"No sir, Chief McRae. I waited and talked to the ER physician, Dr. Abraham. I believe he tried everything possible to save her though."

"I'm sure he did." The slender man sat down beside her. "Do we need to talk? I heard she begged you to go along in the ambulance. Personally, I believe it was the right decision. I'm glad you did."

Terri forced a slight smile. "The doctor asked me to contact the next of kin. Did our guys find any identification in the wreckage? We can get the police to run a 10-28 to get more information. Did the cops who worked it find anything? Heck, I could go through the rubble, help the forensic team if you'd like. Or perhaps …"

"Neal, you're rambling. We ran the license plate. It came back to a white female, age 22, Cilia K. Wisner on Beckley Avenue. I contacted the family myself. Don't worry about the details, okay? You already did more than your share."

"God, I forgot she told me her name." Both hands covered her face.

"Listen, for a moment I thought I saw your ol' daddy out there."

"You, you were on the scene?"

"The passion showed. I heard you shouting out instructions. Plus, it was your dogged ardor and actions that freed the girl."

"But did I do enough?"

"You're an excellent, experienced firefighter; don't ever doubt it. Your best is your best. I can't ask for more." He glanced at his watch. "It's late. Head on in. Call it a night, okay? If there's a problem sleeping, you can always call me, no matter the hour. We're family, remember?"

She looked into his gray eyes. They matched the silver at his temples. Close to her father's age, the intensity of a stressful career was evident on the man's face. "What about the paperwork, sir?"

"Our part is finished and filed away. Now, go home and don't argue." He stood. "You've got comp time. Why not use some of it? Get away for a while. The City Secretary will gripe and moan if you roll over a whole month at the end of the year, especially since you're the only female firefighter on the payroll. Not to mention, the City Manager loves to nit-pick. Make my job easier and take a break."

For the second time tonight, Frank's words echoed. *Have some real fun for a change.* "Okay, but don't blame me if those guys get all the files and reports screwed up while I'm gone."

Chief McRae walked toward the doorway and paused. "One thing's for sure, they can't compare to you, Neal."

CHAPTER FOUR

Crickets chirped a syncopated rhythm as Frank locked the door to the Short Cut Bar and Grill. A glance toward the heavens revealed a rhinestone, star-sprinkled sky. *What a weird night. After wrestling the old mop around, my back hurts, and my knee throbs like a jackhammer.*

Thoughts of the feisty brunette emerged. *I wanted to tell Terri about the new guy who comes in, but I guess she don't need an old man's advice.* The key slipped into his pants pocket. *What am I thinking? Maybe I should just sell the bar and retire.*

In the pale orange glow of a nearby security light, the building stood before him like an old friend. "Crap, can't remember if I locked the storage door after I put up the mop bucket," he grumbled. Absorbed in thought, he didn't hear the crunch of gravel. Something hard jabbed his side.

"Jeest open the door, and let's go right back in."

Frank recognized the deep husky voice. "Look, no one filed charges. Why not forget what happened, okay? No harm, no foul?"

The barrel of a gun gouged deeper into his ribcage. Frank caught his breath as the hammer clicked.

"I could blow you away and be gone in five seconds. So, do what I say. It'd be morning 'fore anyone found a dead, bloody body with bugs crawling all over it. Now, unlock the door!"

Hands shaking, the key turned in the lock. Frank flipped on the light and spun, speechless at the face before him.

18

"How ya like my new nose piece?" the man pointed to a wide bandage. "Don't cha know who I am?"

"How could I forget? You're Orin Chambers. When you first came in tonight, you acted as if you didn't want me to say, so I played along. Man, it really scared me when that mug busted on the floor." Frank laughed nervously.

"You always were a lousy liar. Don't think I didn't recognize the snooty slut, too. She's Chuck Neal's illegitimate kid." Orin shook the gun in the direction where Terri sat earlier.

"What ... what do you mean illegitimate?"

"Oh my. Are ya skeered she might be mine? Hell, I tracked down that scank's mama when I came back to town years ago, but couldn't make it to first base." The gun poked Frank's chest.

"Hey Orin, we're good. Put away the hardware, okay? I ain't no threat."

"Oh, so we're good, huh? Wanna know why I threw the mug? I was pissed. Wanna know why I was pissed?" The weapon continued to prod.

"Guess 'cause of bad service. Sorry." Frank tried to chuckle, but nerves made him cough.

"It weren't about no stupid service, moron. I heard ya'll talking about Nam. You lying dog. You ain't never been to Nam, and that bum knee is a souvenir from doing time in the pokey—for little ol' *me*." A wide grin revealed crooked, yellow teeth accompanied by foul breath. "How'd you like for me to worm myself right into that fancy brunette's life?"

Frank tried to stay calm. "Look man, we both know you set me up. I never stole a thing, but you left me to be the fall guy. I shouldn't have ever crossed the state line, but how was I supposed to know it was a getaway car? Precious time was wasted in prison for something I didn't do. All my friends went to college or signed up to fight in the war. Coming back to this gossipy old town, I needed a good story. Give me some credit—I talked big and lied a lot."

"Well, since we're having a little heart-to-heart, I wanna know how you got the sentence down to eighteen months? Did you promise the Judge in Atlanta to kiss his ...?"

"Don't be vulgar, Orin. I told the *truth*, and Judge Saylors believed me. He realized I was a victim, drunk in the passenger seat, and guilty only by association. The man gave me a second chance. Still, I wasted a portion of my life for you, who ran off into the woods."

Orin grabbed Frank's shirt and pointed the gun in his face. "Ya see any crocodile tears in my eyes? I heard you fessed up, so heroic and all. They found my fingerprints in the car when it came back stolen and arrested me a couple weeks later. I did time upstate. So, don't expect any sympathy." His eyes narrowed. "After a while, I got smart and made a little deal. In return, they put me in the military, a new program to rehabilitate mean old boogiemen like me. The last year of my sentence, I marched around in heavy fatigues and war gear at a boot camp. All work and no glory." He coughed up a wad of spit, and it landed on the hardwood floor. "Only good thing is I can go to the VA hospital for stupid stuff."

"I ... I really didn't know. I mean, how could I?"

"Yeah? What about the rest of the story?"

"What do you mean?"

"Aw, don't leave out the part about when ya come back and your best buddy done got hitched up with your girlfriend, knocked her up, and had a kid. How'd that sit in your craw? Heard all about if from some waggin' tongues." Orin released the grip and started to laugh.

"Why not put the gun away? Do you need money or a place to sleep? I don't mind helping out a pal."

"You damn right you're gonna help me out. Open up the storage room and get me some grub. Where's the cash from the till? Somebody's gonna pay for the damages I suffered tonight and the crappy fine. If it ain't your girly friend, then it's gonna be you."

"Sure, sure give me a second. The bank bag is over by my jacket. You can have it. I'll make up a story — tell everybody I was robbed, and the guy got away. How's that sound?"

"Sounds *too* good, you old scab." He stuck the gun to Frank's temple. "Can't take a chance on you spilling the beans."

Brilliant sparks of red and yellow flew from the barrel of the gun. The room went black.

A hollow ring filled Frank's ears. The timbre bellowed until he wanted to scream. Searing pain ripped through his body. His legs buckled. The floor felt cold, hard, and sticky. *Where is everyone? Did they all go home?* The room spun like a top, faster and faster. *How'd I get on a merry-go-round? All the horses are after me, or am I chasing them?*

CHAPTER FIVE

In the driveway of 605 Jasper Lane, the engine of the Jeep rumbled to a halt. Terri stared at her childhood home. The three-bedroom bungalow Chuck Neal built still exuded timeless charm, social dignity, and warm character. The slanted roof and recessed dormers resembled an adult-size dollhouse with gingerbread trim and bay windows. Giant live oaks, garnished by wispy tails of moss, framed the front yard. Pink phlox and yellow primrose cuddled around robust camellia bushes across the edge of the porch, another reminder of her father's handiwork.

Paused at the top of the steps, a slight breeze carried the sweet smell of honeysuckle. The photocell lamplight popped on, and amber rays caressed the semi-circle porch. *Home sweet home.* Memories of playing baseball with her dad, or curled up by his side in the old wooden porch swing, induced a pang of loneliness. Nothing in life seemed the same since his death.

"Veteran Firefighter's Death Remains a Mystery."

Terri never believed the story. *My daddy had a quick mind, could see the big picture in an instant. He would never go into a burning building unprepared.* A few naysayers swore it was suicide. *No way!*

The key clicked in the slot of the beveled glass door. Quick fingers punched in the code to disarm the alarm. *The last thing I want is a throng of cop cars in the neighborhood.*

"Hello LC." A yellow tabby cat sat near the entrance. Terri turned on the light and tossed the keys on the coffee table. "How was your day? It had to be better than mine."

The cat purred as if to reply.

She dropped down on the pale green couch and stuffed a throw pillow behind her head. Her neck hurt. In fact, her whole body ached, but the image of Parker's swagger brought a slight smile. He'd asked her out a couple times. Sandy blond hair and tawny colored eyes labeled him a definite Adonis. However, her daddy's words of caution couldn't be denied. *Keep a locked gate between work and pleasure.* They met off duty a few times at the Short Cut for a drink, but it ended there.

A rumble erupted in her stomach. "Guess the salad I ate at lunch is long gone, LC." She walked over and stroked the cat sprawled on a large braided rug in front of the fireplace. "Want to join me in the kitchen?"

The door to the pantry creaked open. "Man, I need to buy some groceries." The small brown package easily ripped open, and she poured the contents into a cup of water. "Instant oatmeal will have to do." The microwave beeped, and a curl of steam rose from the hot cereal. As she reached inside the refrigerator for butter, her cell phone rang. "This is Neal. What? Oh my God, no!"

◆◆◆◆

The automated doors at Griffin County Hospital barely parted before Terri squeezed through. Tears threatened to tumble as she sprinted down the hall. Rounding the corner toward the emergency room, a pair of muscular arms halted the progress.

"Whoa, be careful." Two hands gripped her shoulders.

She stared into the handsome face of Sergeant Green. "Parker, what are you doing here?"

"I responded for backup at the Short Cut. Who called you?"

"I, I don't know—someone from dispatch at the PD. They said something happened to Frank. Where is he? Can I see him?"

"Hey sweetheart, slow down, and I'll tell you what I know." He led her to some vacant chairs. "Take a seat."

"No. Tell me about Frank."

"Okay, remember Mr. Higgins, the old guy who lives about a block down from the bar? He's forever calling in noise complaints on Frank. Well, seems he went out to let his bulldog take a piss, uh sorry, I mean pee. Anyway, he heard a gun go off."

"What?" A hand flew to her chest.

"Dispatch reported shots fired. Ray Grimes was in the area and responded first. Good thing Higgins made the call as soon as he did or ..."

"Or what?"

"Firefighter Neal? You're not in uniform. Are you off duty?"

Terri turned to face the dark blue eyes and infectious smile that calmed her nerves hours before.

"You know Ms. Firefighter, we've got to stop meeting like this." He wagged a finger.

A grin formed as she stood between the cop and the doctor.

Each man stared at the other.

"I would have preferred to have kept the date we talked about earlier tonight."

Parker cocked an eyebrow. "What date?"

"Dr. Abraham, I need to know about Frank Gunnison."

"Please, call me Tucker. Are you kin to Mr. Gunnison?"

"No, but he's like an uncle to me. He has no other family. How is he? Can I see him? Is he going to be okay? What happened?" She fought hard not to cry.

"I'd say he's a very lucky man in more ways than one. First, to have you care so much about him, and second, the fact the bullet passed cleanly through. It would've done a lot more damage a few centimeters inward."

"Bullet? He was shot?" Sourness churned at the sound of the words. *How could this happen to someone like Frank? Dear Frank, sweet Frank?*

"I've already got the information from Grimes, Terri," Parker interjected.

She grabbed his uniform sleeve. "What happened? Don't lie. I want to know." Her eyes darted between the two men. "Both of you are keeping something from me." Exhaustion and frustration gave way to tears.

The doctor put a hand on her shoulders and forced her to sit down. "I think your patrolman here can explain the details."

"It's Sergeant, Sergeant Green." Parker pointed to the name badge.

"Okay ... Sergeant Green. I'm going back into the emergency room, Terri. When I get Mr. Gunnison settled, I'll come get you, okay?"

She nodded and wiped away tears with the back of her hand. He called her *Terri,* and she liked it. For a moment, his voice seemed to sooth the panic. "Parker, I can't stand much more. Tell me the truth," her voice broke.

The officer sat down and took her hand. "I'll tell you all I know, just please calm down."

She offered a slight nod.

"When Grimes arrived on the scene, the front door to the Short Cut was partially open and dark inside. He heard a groan and found Frank on the floor in a pool of blood. The guy mumbled something about being mugged and robbed. The cash drawer was empty and no bank bag in sight. The forensic team will have to tell us the rest of the story." Parker paused. "Do you want something to eat or drink? I've never seen you this pale, Terri."

"No, no. What happened next? Is that it?"

"Well, they rushed Frank into emergency surgery, and I guess your doctor *friend* operated on him."

A tide of fatigue gushed, and she slumped.

"Hey, Frank is a tough old bird. He'll pull through and be more ornery than ever." Parker gently kissed her forehead.

Maybe I misjudged Parker. Although extremely independent, right now she needed someone to coddle her, reassure her. Kiss it, and make it all better.

"I think you need some coffee. I sure could use a cup. Stay here. I'll go to the cafeteria. Why don't you rest your eyes while I'm gone?" He stood.

"Thanks. Coffee does sound good, but if you need to go back on patrol, it's okay. You don't have to stay."

"Yeah, yeah, you say that now, and then in a week or so, it'll be all over the PD I was an inconsiderate bum. No, no, not gonna play your little game, woman." He winked and walked away.

Eyes closed, she tried to settle her nerves. *I have to admit, this softer side of the sergeant is very attractive, even sexy.*

"Terri?"

"Yes, Dr. Abraham? I mean, Tucker." She rose from the chair.

One corner of his mouth pulled to a slight smile. "I like the way you say my name."

She felt her pulse race.

"Frank will be in room 323 in a few minutes. It's fine to go up there. However, he's heavily sedated. If he mumbles or appears incoherent, don't be alarmed. He might float in and out of consciousness for a good while. Seeing how devoted you are, I asked the head nurse to provide a rollaway bed. The best thing to do for your uncle is to get some rest. Deal?" He placed his hands on her shoulders once more, and her knees buckled. He quickly steadied her. "Do you want a wheelchair? Can't have my favorite firefighter fall and expect my attention in the ER, too, now can I?"

"No, really I'm fine. It's just been an unusual and stressful night. That's all. Thanks. Room 323, right?" She turned in the direction of the elevator, but stopped. "Oh, Sergeant Green went to the cafeteria for some coffee. Can you explain things to him?"

"I'd be happy to take care of the cop for you." He pulled her near and gave a slight hug. "See you in the morning."

CHAPTER SIX

A muffled resonance from the hallway filtered into the hospital room. Terri stood rigid at the sight before her. In musical precision, the constant beep of the monitors displayed Frank's vital signs. Medical paraphernalia, tubes, and IVs took on the appearance of a tangled spider web. Bandages covered his head and left shoulder. A large plum colored bruise covered his right cheek. Butterfly stitches on his forehead, nose, and chin, distorted his face. Dr. Abraham said Frank might have hit the counter, fell to the floor, and received a concussion. However, to Terri everything else was secondary compared to the bullet wound.

One small step at a time, she approached. The man in the bed looked pallid, lifeless. A tender touch to his brow whisked her back to the day her daddy died ... sadness, emptiness, fear.

Thank you, Lord. At least, Frank is alive. "You *will* be okay. Tucker promised."

She tried to focus on the rhythmic rise and fall of Frank's chest, but weariness enveloped all concentration. The sight of the temporary bed brought a grateful sigh. Rest would be essential to handle this dreadful situation.

"To tell the truth, I can't wait to hear you cuss up a storm wanting to know when you can go home, Frank," she whispered. Soft lips brushed his rough cheek. "You're such a big part of my life, you grumpy old man. We'll see this through together. Don't worry. I'll always be close by."

TASTE OF FIRE

After a silent prayer, she slipped off her shoes and slid under the covers of the rollaway bed. The rock-hard pillow didn't matter; exhaustion prompted sleep.

◆◆◆◆

The shrill sound of a siren made Terri sit straight up. "What, uh, where am I?" Memories tumbled like puzzle pieces—the explosion, the girl in the mangled car, the cries for help. *Where did she go? Did I dream it?*

Outside the room, hospital chatter brought back the sting of reality.

The older man looked so helpless; eyes open in a half slit.

Barefooted, she clung to the metal rail. "Frank?"

A young nurse entered the room, a caddy filled with glass vials in her hand. "Time to take blood. Do you want to go get something to eat or drink and give me a little time with your dad?" The girl pulled a cord, and the bright light broke the semi-darkness.

Terri squinted and fumbled for her shoes. "Uh, he's not my dad. Sorta like my uncle."

"I see. Well, I only need a few minutes, and he's all yours again."

Terri recalled Parker's offer. "I'll be right back. I'm going for some coffee, so be nice while I'm gone." She patted Frank's arm.

He didn't respond.

Downstairs, an older woman tended a large aluminum urn. "Griffin County Hospital Volunteer" was embroidered in red script on the blue striped smock. "Good morning, hon."

"Morning? Goodness, what time is it?"

"Oh, the sun will be up in a bit. Would you like some coffee? Fresh made." The woman offered a Styrofoam cup.

TASTE OF FIRE

"Thanks, smells great."

"I'm Margie, but if you want a bite to eat, Gladys has warm bagels at her post near the end of this hall." She pointed. "Dear me, you need some meat on your bones, little girl. Go tell Gladys Margie sent you and be sure to get jelly. Oh, the apple butter is scrumptious. Gotta eat to keep up your strength. Understand?"

"Yes ma'am. I appreciate this." The steamy liquid warmed her hand. She thought about the uneaten oatmeal on the kitchen counter. *No doubt, LC has helped himself by now.*

Chatty Gladys insisted Terri take several packages of jelly because, after all, they *were* free. She couldn't help but chuckle at the robust, insistent hospital volunteer.

In a nearby waiting area, Terri sat next to a window. A trace of sunlight peeked through thick azure clouds and illuminated the sky. Leaves on a nearby silver leaf maple shimmered in the early breeze. *Looks like a beautiful day. I wish Frank could see it. Gosh, I've taken so many blessings for granted.*

The second day passed in a haze while Terri watched nurse after nurse go through their duties of blood pressure and temperature checks, replacement of the IV, recording the monitor information, and redressing the bandages. Idle conversations brought a sense of comfort as the attendants assumed she was a daughter of the patient.

Still unresponsive, Frank appeared comatose.

"You might as well be my daddy." Terri caressed his limp hand.

"Like I said before, Mr. Gunnison is a very lucky man."

Startled, Terri looked toward the door and into the cobalt eyes of Dr. Abraham. "I thought you said you would check on Frank daily. It's almost midnight. You haven't shown your face since they put him in this room—two days ago. Where have you been?" A frown formed.

"There were multiple surgeries on my schedule, but I've called the head nurse before each shift change since he was admitted to check his status ... and yours." Tucker walked to her side.

"Me? Don't worry about me. Worry about the patient you promised would be okay. Look at him. He doesn't move, or open his eyes, or speak a word, or ... even know I'm here." Both hands struck Tucker's chest as fear gave way to sobs.

Arms encased her shaking frame. "Shhh, I know this is scary, but Frank's body is in a defensive mode, a natural healing process. That's a good sign."

Terri found strength in the touch of his hand as he lifted her chin.

Their eyes connected.

Those memorable eyes. She stifled a sudden urgent desire to kiss the doctor.

"Give Frank more time. I don't break my promises." He eased her down onto the rollaway bed. "All my patients are important to me, and so are you."

Frustration dissolved, and she stretched out on the makeshift bed. He pulled the sheet up to her waist, squeezed her hand, and walked to the door.

The intercom blared, "Doctor Abraham, Doctor Abraham. Report to the ER. Dr. Abraham."

"After my mid-morning rounds, I'll be back. Goodnight, but if you need me, I'm only a page away. All the nurses on this floor have been given written orders to accommodate your needs. I suggest you take advantage of it."

A vision of them in a passionate embrace emerged. *No, don't go there.*

The third day dawned.

Terri took the plastic bag filled with clothes and sundries Parker brought on his last visit and locked the bathroom door. *I need a hot shower before my usual routine of coffee from Margie and a bagel from Gladys.*

Walking back into Frank's room with a towel twisted on her head, she didn't notice the nearby silhouette.

"Man, you smell good."

The towel fell to the floor, and wet tousled hair tumbled to her shoulders. "Tucker, you scared me."

"Sorry, but looks like I'm just in time." He retrieved the cloth.

"Excuse me?"

"I don't see a cup of Margie's famous fresh brewed coffee or one of Gladys' to-die-for bagels anywhere." He smiled.

"What? How did you know …?"

"Your daily routine? I have my sources. Besides, I said I care about you, which brings me to the reason why I'm here. Let's go have breakfast." An arm linked in hers.

"But my hair—it's wet."

"Yes and very becoming the way those ebony curls frame your face." He turned her toward the door.

"Wait. No. I can't leave here. Maybe some other time." She pulled back.

"Terri, I meant the hospital cafeteria. I'm smart enough to know you won't leave Frank. Come on."

TASTE OF FIRE

An hour later, the elevator door opened on the third floor. The couple stepped out, hand in hand, and stopped in front of room 323.

"Ms. Neal, thank you for the pleasure of your company." Tucker kissed the top of her hand.

She shook her head and laughed. "You definitely know how to make me smile."

"Good. You have a beautiful one, and I want to see more of it, okay?"

"Gosh, I haven't thanked you for the extra bed. Please, forgive me."

"It's pretty noisy around here most of the time, but you do look more rested. There's a new sparkle in your eyes today. I'd like to think I contributed somehow."

"Oh ... yes, you did ... I mean," Terri stuttered.

"Excuse me, Dr. Abraham." A man in blue scrubs held a tray of food.

"Sure, Mark." Tucker pushed open the door. "Looks like the dietary staff has Frank fixed up."

"Goodness, there's coffee, juice, scrambled eggs, and biscuits. Smells good," Terri replied.

"Yup, and I'm not even hungry." Tucker winked.

"If only Frank would wake up and get some nourishment." She shrugged.

"With all this dang noise, how's a fella supposed to get any cotton pickin' rest?" a hoarse voice whispered.

Terri ran into the room. "Oh Frank, you're awake! Thank God. I'm so glad. Here, let me fix this." She opened a packet of sugar and emptied it in the cup.

"What're ya doing? I don't use sissy stuff in my coffee. Black—you know I drink it black." Frank tried to reposition himself, but grimaced.

"Hey, don't get wild on me, old man. You're not in any shape to bark out a bunch of orders this morning. I'll drink this one and get you another. How about it?"

"Leave it. Might do me good to try something new, I guess."

"The important thing is to eat and get some strength back."

"What I *need* is out of this place. Where's the doctor?" Frank mumbled.

"Tucker is right here."

"You know him?" He raised an eyebrow.

Tucker stepped up to the bed. "Yes, I guess you could say we've spent some time together lately. Now, Mr. Gunnison ..."

"Aw Doc, you know I don't like that 'Mister' stuff."

"Well Frank, it sounds like you're on the road to recovery." Tucker chuckled. "Perhaps your stay will be a short one if you continue to improve every day."

"Yes, he's getting back to his sweet grumpy self," Terri added.

"Well, I might not be grumpy if someone would roll the tray over so I could eat some breakfast. Geez, what's a guy gotta do for a little food? Dance a jig?"

"See what I mean?" Terri shook her head.

"Yes, I believe I'm beginning to understand. Frank, I'll have the nurse come inspect the incision after you finish eating. Expect me back to check on the both of you."

"Before you leave, please update him about the bump on his head and the bullet wound," Terri said.

"And when can I go home? I got a business to run, ya know."

TASTE OF FIRE

"How many times have you said you never have any time off? Welcome to Griffin County Hospital, your new vacation spot." She patted his hand.

Frank tried to cross his arms, but the bandage got in the way.

"The MRI shows a slight concussion. We need to keep you a while longer to make sure things didn't rattle around too much up there."

Frank pointed at Terri. "No wise cracks."

"Don't tempt me."

"The bullet grazed a bone in your shoulder. It didn't actually penetrate. However, since you lost a large amount of blood, I ordered a transfusion after the surgery." Tucker grabbed Frank's chart from the holder at the end of the bed.

"What? You gave me some dang stranger's blood?" He huffed.

"I can tell you're a handful, Mr. Gunnison." Tucker walked over to Terri. His six-foot stature dwarfed hers.

Charmed by obvious confidence and composure, she felt a ripple of excitement when a hand brushed her arm. *His touch makes me feel safe, secure.*

"Aw geesh. You're back to the 'Mister' stuff again. You got a short memory, Doc."

Tucker laughed. "If you mind the nurses, I bet you can escape this wretched place pretty soon. Tell you what; I'm going to make a note on your chart, some definite orders." He scribbled something and stuck the clipboard under his arm.

"Orders? What kind of orders?" Frank pursed his lips.

"Strict orders, Frank," Tucker replied. "Terri is in charge."

35

CHAPTER SEVEN

"Well, ain't this a dandy deal? You have to spend day and night at the dang hospital, and now gotta feed me? I ain't no invalid, you know." Frank wrinkled his nose.

"Eat your lunch, Mr. Sunshine. I only buttered the roll. It's only been a few days. Don't fuss so much. Besides, we're family. Tucker visits on a regular basis, most of the hospital staff knows me by name, and the volunteers have tried to fatten me up. Thanks to you, I've become pretty famous." Terri tucked a paper napkin in the neck of Frank's hospital gown. "Since you're more coherent, and able to communicate better today, I want to know exactly what happened at the Short Cut."

"Uh, didn't the cops tell you?" He jerked the napkin out.

"Parker told me Ray Grimes responded to a shots fired call from a disgruntled neighbor down the street. What do you remember?"

"Geeze, it's still kinda fuzzy."

"Take your time, young man. I'm not about to leave." She crossed her arms.

"Okay, well, uh." He rolled his eyes. "Yeah, I decided to go back inside to see if I locked the storage room." He took a sip of coffee. "Guess the door was left ajar. Maybe someone drove by, saw it open, and decided it'd be a good time to rob the place."

"Oh good grief, you were shot, for heaven's sake. Didn't you hear a voice or get a glimpse of their face? Were they wearing a mask, did you even *see* the gun?

Can't you remember more?" Both hands flew as the questions tumbled.

"Well, I'm not real sure how I got shot. They hit me from behind. It hurt like the dickens, and everything went black. Guess they left me for dead." He took a bite and watched as she twisted a long curl. From the intense expression, he knew to choose each word carefully. "Are ya gonna analyze everything I say?"

"Frank, don't you realize how much I care? For pity's sake, I love you." Tears filled her eyes.

"Aw little T, I'm gonna be okay, sorry. Heck, you know I love you, too—ever since you were a twig. Doc is gonna fix me up good. Besides, I promised to do what you and him say so I can get out of here. Please don't cry."

She sniffed. "Oh my stars, you haven't called me Little T in years."

"Hey, I ain't going nowhere. Please don't fret. You're the one who needs a break. All them long, hard hours at a stressful job will make ya old before your time."

She sat at the end of the bed. "Funny you should say that because the Chief mentioned I needed to use some of my comp time."

"There ya go. Do it. Get away for a while."

"Oh, I could never leave, Frank. No way. Not now, especially with you in the hospital." A hand went up in protest.

"Listen young lady, Doc said you were in charge of me. He didn't say I couldn't be in charge of you, too." A thin grin formed.

"Eat your food, and don't be silly," she replied.

"I may be old, with a big bump on my head, and a shot up shoulder, but I *do* remember I suggested you needed a change."

"What are you talking about? I think you were hit harder on the head than we thought."

"Yeah, well see if you recall this. When I mentioned you needed to do something crazy for a change, you bolted outta the Short Cut like a frightened rabbit. Remember?"

Terri grinned and shook her head.

"See there, I knew it." He pointed the fork at her.

"Knew what?" She stood. "I smiled, that's all, a silly smile."

"Look Little T, I'll be outta here in a couple days, so start making some plans."

◆◆◆◆

Frank relaxed in his old recliner and watched Terri scribble on a notepad.

"The home health agency called. A nurse will come here to your house three times a week to redress the bandage on your shoulder, and Meals-At-Home stop by twice a day to make sure you have plenty to eat. In addition, the administrator assured me their nurses will be glad to prepare a pot of coffee, brew a pitcher of tea, or make some sandwiches if you like." She wrapped a blanket across his knees. "I organized all your prescription bottles on the side table by your chair and made a list of how often to take them. The nurses monitor the medication schedule, so don't forget."

"Uh, let me see ... I know I had something else to say." She bit down on the pen and stared toward the ceiling. "Oh yes, some of the guys at the station put up a sign at the Short Cut to let people know you're closed for a while. Parker requested extra patrol because, after all, it's still a crime scene. Since most of the town knows, you may have phone calls and visitors. Company might be good, just please don't over do it." Terri kissed his cheek. "Also, Dr. Abraham called. He's attending a conference in Mobile, but said he'll phone to check on you daily."

"All this commotion ain't necessary, I tell ya." Frank sighed.

"Oh come on, you love it." She knelt beside him. "You do know I would never leave if I didn't think you could function alone for a couple days, right?"

"Sure, so where ya going?"

"I haven't really made up my mind, but got a couple ideas. Here's my cell phone number if anything were to happen."

He took the piece of paper and stuck it in his left shirt pocket. "Ya seem pretty cheery, and that makes me feel better. Now, skedaddle. Ain't nothing gonna happen."

"I have to admit, I'm a little excited about this road trip." Suitcase in hand, Terri headed to the door. "The question is ... can I trust you to behave until I get back?"

Frank waved. "Leave already, or do I have to get up from here and get a switch?"

CHAPTER EIGHT

Wind whipped through Terri's hair as she sped along in the yellow '66 Mustang convertible. The sun glinted off the laminated, wood grain steering wheel, and she ran a finger across it. Time spent with her father restoring the pony car, as well as an old work jeep, brought a rush of pleasant memories. Thoughts drifted to the day he asked about a paint job.

"I want it to be canary yellow."
Chuck laughed. "What? And have it look like Big Bird?"
"Oh Daddy, you know he was my favorite character. Yup, yellow it is, and Big Bird is what I'll call it."

A punch to the gas pedal, and the gauge quickly pegged out. *Nothing like a little acceleration for an adrenalin fix.* The rhythmic drone of the motor reminded her of past vacations. She glanced at the passenger's seat. *I know you're riding with me Daddy. You always do.*

Convinced Frank would be okay, she relaxed and listened to the hum of the tires on the asphalt. His advice to do something crazy brought a grin.

At the edge of Atlanta, shades of peach and amber floated on the horizon of a dusky blue sky.

Terri exited off the interstate into the parking lot of the Montero Suites. The glass lobby door chimed as she entered.

Behind the counter, a young man in a white shirt and striped blue tie typed on a computer. "Welcome to your home away from home," he greeted.

"Thanks. I don't have a reservation. Do you have a non-smoking room available? I'd prefer downstairs, too."

Taste of Fire

"Well, for someone as pretty as you, I *might* be able to make it happen." His smile produced a shiny row of metal braces.

Terri pulled out her American Firefighter Association card. "Nice try, honey, but you're a bit too young. By the way, I want my 20% discount."

Settled into the hotel room, she thumbed through the yellow pages of a thick phone book. A finger stopped on a large half-page ad. "Yeah, this place sounds perfect. After a hot bath, I'll be ready to roll." The book tumbled onto the bed.

Hot water churned the frothy bubble bath. Misty steam obscured the mirrors as she slid down beneath the pearly paradise. A deep breath escaped. *I did need some time away. This is heaven.* A hand traced the curves of her body and rested for a moment on the rough misshapen skin of her forearm. Not even thoughts of the scar could dishearten the agenda. She often referred to it as her 'stripes'. Given the right situation, she'd roll up a sleeve and challenge other colleagues to prove they could *fool* the fire, too.

Opaque bubbles clung to shapely hips as Terri stepped out of the tub and grabbed a thick, white towel. The full-length mirror caught the image. *Curves and muscle, too. Looks like those long hours in the Station House gym did pay off.*

A couple of raven curls hung loose. She took the hair clip out and moved closer to the mirror, eyes locked on the scar. Thoughts of cruel remarks from kids in school rekindled an old embarrassment.

Her father's tender description emerged once again to ease the anguish.

It was a rain slick night when Mommy put you and your bear in the car to run an errand. She forgot she drank some bad medicine earlier, and it made her sleepy. She couldn't control the car. It ran off the road, crashed into a tree, and burst into flames. The fire jumped all around you and licked your arm to get a taste. Because you didn't cry, the fire was afraid and realized how special and tough you are.

Years later, Terri realized the bad medicine referenced was whiskey. Maybe that explained why she could handle her liquor now—thanks to Mama. A sudden anger lit her dark eyes as she stared at the reflection. "Well, to abandon me and Daddy was not the answer." Fingers patted perfumed lotion over the rough, disfigured skin. "Just let someone say something, anything, about it tonight."

The zipper of the suitcase buzzed. She slipped on a short, black skirt with fringed hem. The cropped, apricot halter fit mid waist and showed just enough skin to tease the onlookers. "This is pretty dang cute, and a perfect match to my new coral-colored Fatbaby boots."

A western station blared on the clock radio while she finished applying makeup. Car keys in hand, she headed out to 'do something crazy'.

Skirts & Spurs flashed in bright yellow neon above an old renovated warehouse.

The sports car pulled into the entrance and stopped. Inside the dancehall, country music thumped a three-quarter beat waltz as she closed the car door.

At the entry, a stocky-built cowboy let out a slow wolf whistle and nodded.

Arm out stretched, Terri dangled the keys. "Are you the valet?"

"I'm anything you need me to be, ma'am. My name is Weston. Welcome to Skirts and Spurs." Two dimples appeared through a wide smile.

TASTE OF FIRE

"Well, then ... *Weston*, take good care of my pony." She winked.

Inside, a crush of couples rubbed belt buckles and two-stepped across the huge wooden floor. Rusty, corrugated metal walls sported cow skulls, ropes, and wagon wheels. In one corner, a mechanical bull beckoned to the brave for a ride. Western memorabilia hung overhead from rough timber beams throughout the expansive club.

Weaving through the crowd, she walked pass the bar at the front of the building and headed to a smaller one in the back.

"Need something to drink, honey?" an older woman behind the counter hollered above the music.

"Corona and two slices of lime." Terri wiggled in between two girls wearing cut-off jean shorts and placed a five-dollar bill on the counter.

"Here ya go, sweetie. Let me get ya some change."

"Keep it," Terri said.

"Thanks much. You're new here aren't ya?"

She leaned closer to the bartender. The woman's thick black hair was twisted on top of her head in a silver clip. Onyx eyes gleamed like two pieces of coal. Terri guessed the lady was in her fifty's by the laugh lines and light crow's feet. However, a firm figure belied the age.

"You're pretty good to notice a new face in a crowd like this." Terri opened her mouth and squeezed the limes. The bitter juice made her grit her teeth.

"Comes from over twenty-five years in the bartending business. Ain't that a trophy to put on a resume?" The woman slapped the counter.

Terri settled on a barstool. "Pretty neat place here."

"Yeah, I guess so. Seems to get louder every night though, or maybe I'm getting hard of hearing. I'd like to think I could stay forever young, but ain't that a joke?" She laughed. "Hey, everyone around here calls me Mom."

"That's cool, but why?"

"Goodness darlin', 'cause I've been around since the wranglers rode in on dinosaurs. Damned old fossils hated those spurs, too ... I mean the dinosaurs, not the cowboys." She shook her head. "How about you? Got a name?"

Terri hesitated for a moment. Images of the mess at the Short Cut Bar and Grill came to mind. *"Geeze Louise, did you cause all this mess Terri Neal?"*

"Louise," Terri replied. "But my friends call me Lou." She took a sip.

"Nice to meet you, Lou."

The music ended, and someone at the microphone announced to the crowd, "The band is gonna take a break. Who wants to put some coins in the juke box and line dance?"

A squeal erupted from a group of young girls who rushed forward.

"Why don't you go find a cowboy and break a heart?" Mom pointed toward the dance floor.

"Not just yet, I've got something else in mind." She chugged down the beer and left the bottle on the counter.

"Whatever you say, Lou."

"See ya in a bit." Terri gave a thumb up and headed toward the stage.

One of the band members knelt beside an amplifier.

"Think it would be okay if I did a spotlight?"

He looked up and chuckled. "Uh, did you say you needed a flashlight?"

"You *are* a real cowboy aren't you?" Terri grinned.

"Yes ma'am, I am." He stood and straightened the pewter-colored Stetson. Wisps of black hair curled around his ears. His frame was lean, yet muscular, and the jeans fit tight with a starched line down each leg.

"Look, I thought I might take the stage when the band comes back to do a spotlight, and I don't need a flashlight."

"Oh, I see. You want to karaoke." A thumb hooked in one of the belt loops.

"Look dude, there's a big difference in a solo and singing along with a stupid disc, but if your band ... what's it called?"

"Mama's Sons—our band is called Mama's Sons. Don't tell me you ain't ever heard of us? We opened last month for ..."

"Like I said, if your band isn't up to it, no big deal." She spun on a heel.

"Hey Miss, wait. I'm sorry. Didn't mean to offend you. My band can play whatever you can sing, and by the way, I'm Wade. I like it a whole bunch better than *dude*. Now, who are you?" He took off the felt hat and did an exaggerated bow. A ring haloed around dark hair. He ran a hand through it, and replaced the hat.

"Lou," Terri said.

"Pretty name for a pretty lady," he replied.

She whispered in his ear and took a step back to watch the expression.

Light brown eyes brighten. "Heck, sure ... sounds like fun. Let me tell the guys."

A single beam hit center stage where Terri stood, and the chatter of the crowd hushed.

Taste of Fire

At Wade's nod, Mama's Sons rocked the sensual bluesy tune, Black Velvet.

Terri crooned the lyrics and worked the crowd while the fringe on the short skirt swished to the rhythm.

After the song ended, she pointed to a burly guy with a goatee and crooked a finger. "Hey, come join me."

The patrons whooped as he straightened his straw cowboy hat and jumped upon the platform.

"What's your name, cowboy." A hand grabbed the front of his plaid shirt.

"Uh, Tex, ma'am."

"Well, Tex ... ready to have some fun?" She released the grasp.

"Shore 'nuff." He tapped his hat.

The drummer hit a four count, and Terri went straight into Before He Cheats with the amenable cowboy. At the end of the song, Tex fell to the stage floor, and she propped a boot on his back. The crowd broke into laughter at the animation. After the invitee finally stood, Terri gave him a hug.

Wade announced, "Let's hear it for Lou and Tex, everybody." He took her hand and held it up. "You want more?"

The audience clapped and shouted for an encore, but she shook her head, blew Wade a kiss, and stepped off the stage.

A mass of people clamored around for an autograph as two bouncers flanked her. Reluctantly, Terri obliged the newfound bevy of fans, thanked them, and headed to the back bar.

Mom stood, mouth agape. "Didn't know you were somebody famous, hon. What a show."

TASTE OF FIRE

"Thanks, just having some fun. I've never done anything like that before."

"My goodness child, you musta been holdin' back, and I can't imagine why. You need to give these folks another treat some time. I been tellin' Wade he needs an attraction. Know what I mean? They're my boys, and I love 'em, but they need a girl to spice it up. You'd be perfect."

"That's a great compliment, but Wade will have to find someone else. I had a wild hair tonight. I'm satisfied now."

"Okay young lady, but I believe in your case you *could* quit your day job, whatever it is."

They both laughed.

A flock of hopeful admirers formed a line to dance with Terri. She accepted the first offer and waved to Mom. "Gotta go break a cowboy's heart."

The night slipped into the wee hours of the morning, and by the time she made it back to Mom's counter, her feet hurt, and she was hungry.

"Here." The older woman offered a bottle of water. "You just about burned this place down out there, little girl."

"Gracious sakes, I'm tired." Terri pulled off one boot and wiggled her toes.

"I noticed the twins both twirled you a time or two. Can't say I've ever seen my sons so interested." The woman laughed.

"Twins? They favor some, but I didn't know they were related."

"Fraternal twins—not identical." Mom wiped the counter.

"So, the name of the band is true? Mama's Sons?" Terri drained the bottle of water.

Taste of Fire

"Yup, sure is. Look, it's time for me to leave this high society job. Wanna go for some breakfast?"

"Yes, I'm starved." She forced the boot back on.

"Good, there's a little place down the road open twenty-four hours. A lot of us like to meet there. If you want to go, we can leave out the back door—if you think you can get away from all those fame-hungry patrons."

"Sure," Terri replied. "Thanks for the water. Can I buy you a beer or something before we leave?"

"I don't touch the stuff. Let me clock out, and I'll be ready to go." The cash register clanged shut. "Tell Weston to get your car. I have to count my bag and lock it up. I'll meet you there."

The Red Cup Café boasted a marquee of 'always open'.

Terri waited at the entrance to the restaurant as an older vehicle pulled into the parking lot.

The car coughed like someone with a heavy cigarette addiction. White tufts of smoke puffed from the exhaust.

"One of these days, I'll leave my old junker on the side of the road before it leaves me." Mom said as they went inside.

The crowd was a mixture of customers from truck drivers to teenagers. The clank of dishes rang out through the restaurant, and the smell of fresh brewed coffee taunted Terri. She and Mom waited while a young boy bused a booth in the back.

"Good grief, it feels good to get off my feet for a while." The woman let out a long sigh.

A thin waitress plopped down two menus. "We're swamped right now, it might be a while."

"Girly, we're starved, and you've got at least two more famished cowboys coming. Better punch up those cooks for us," Mom replied.

Terri opened the mummy-wrapped silverware and wiped each utensil with the napkin.

"Who all is coming?"

"Well, Wade and Weston, and maybe even a few from the band, unless they found something better to do than eat." A sly smile formed.

Terri nodded. "Uh, would you care if I asked you a question?"

"Heck yeah, I'll buy your meal. I don't mind."

"Oh no, I have money. In fact, let me treat you," Terri insisted.

"I appreciate it, but we oughta make the boys pay." She scanned the list of choices.

Terri cleared her throat. "What's your real name?"

The older woman peered over the worn menu, eyes narrowed. "Why do you ask? I told you everyone calls me Mom."

"I don't mean to pry ... it just feels a bit odd for me," Terri added.

After a moment of silence, she took the clip from her hair and let it fall to her shoulders. "Loretta, but if you tell anyone I'll have to spank your prissy butt," she whispered. "I never did like my name much."

Terri swallowed hard. "Oh no, it's such, I mean it's really a beautiful name."

"What's wrong, little girl? Your face is pale. Too much liquor? I've got a little pill in my purse to help." She grabbed the handbag and rummaged through it.

"No, I'm not sick, and it's uh, probably only a coincidence." Terri rubbed her forehead.

Taste of Fire

"Lou, I know we only met a few hours ago, but you ain't making much sense, honey. What do you mean a coincidence?"

Taste of Fire
CHAPTER NINE

"Thanks for your help, Danielle." Frank ogled the backside of the petite nurse. *Heck, I may be too old to have such racy thoughts, but then, I ain't dead either.*

"Have a good day, Mr. Gunnison. I'll be back to check on you soon."

The recliner locked into place, and after a couple clicks of the remote, a woman in a red jacket and pearls nodded at the screen. "Thank you for joining us. This is KMJB Channel 2 for around the clock breaking news, headlines, and weather."

"What do ya think you're gonna hear—they found the scum bag who robbed and shot your old butt?"

Frank jumped, suddenly aware of the person behind him. "Orin, I didn't hear you come in."

"Hell no, you didn't hear me. I slipped in the back door. Wouldn't have mattered ... you were too busy checking out the sweet ass of the little nursemaid. I wouldn't mind some pillow talk with that myself." A bulky body moved between Frank and the television, eyes glassy and wide.

"Uh, you want something to eat? There's plenty of food in the kitchen. Those people come by and bring me stuff all the time. You're welcome to any of it." Palms sweaty, Frank kept a calm voice.

"I ain't hungry. What do you think this is—some sorta social call?"

"I just meant ..."

"Shut up! I'm **not** going back to jail. Got it?" Orin grabbed the remote and hit the off button.

"What are you talking about? No one knows it was you who shot me. I told them I was mugged and hit from behind. Didn't see a thing."

"I ain't going back in the slammer with those puke heads. So, ya better make your tale of woe believable." The intimidating image towered above.

On the end table, the cell phone caught Frank's eye. *To try to call for help would be suicidal. This lunatic left me for dead once; he would love it if I tried such a stupid stunt. Gotta regroup.* "Orin, what are you doing here?"

The grungy man dropped down on the couch and propped his dirty military boots on the coffee table. Clumps of dirt sifted downward. "See, the way I got this figured, I need some insurance." He pulled out a toothpick from a torn shirt pocket and probed stained teeth.

"What do you mean by insurance?"

"If you get to feeling a whole bunch better, ya might wanna flap those chops about the other night. Hell, I shoulda made sure you were dead 'fore I left. Why did you try to fight me? What a wimp. The bullet musta hit you and ricocheted off the light. Alls I know, everything went black, and I hauled ass."

"Hey, trust me, I got the message." Frank touched the bandaged shoulder.

"You don't *get* a damn thing," he snarled. "Look at it like a life insurance policy. As long as you pay me, you get to keep livin'." Heinous laughter filled the room.

Fear knotted Frank's stomach, and a vile taste rose in his throat. This thug never showed any signs of a conscience. Killing would come easy.

Suddenly, Orin jumped to his feet. A rough, dirty hand slammed against the damaged shoulder.

A groan gurgled from Frank's lips as pain charged through the wound. His eyes rolled backward.

"Found the tender spot, huh? Right above your old ticker? Shit, I almost took you out, didn't I, buddy?"

The unexpected chime of the doorbell brought an instant reprieve. A shadowy figure waited outside.

"Are things okay here, Frank?" Parker Green opened the screen door.

Orin stepped away, face blanched in the presence of the law officer.

The unexpected opportunity forced composure into Frank's words. "Hello *Mr. Green*, come in. How are you today?" Their friendship spanned many years. Would the cop be sharp enough to catch the little innuendo? Frank fought to suppress the nauseating throb in his shoulder.

Parker walked toward the men. One hand eased closer to the holster. Instead of touching the gun, he wiped a hand on his pant leg and thrust it at the visitor. "Are you a friend of Frank's?"

A rosy pinkness returned to the intruder's face, and they shook hands.

"I'm his uh, cousin. Just happened to come through town. I went by the Short Cut to visit for a while, but a sign said the place is closed for a few days. So, I swung by here to see if Frank was home." Orin stepped around the recliner.

"Really? I didn't see a car out front. Are you on foot?"

"No, no ... came in on a bus and took a cab over here. Wasn't even sure ol' cuz still lived at this address." He turned to Frank. "How long has it been since we seen each other?"

TASTE OF FIRE

Agony racked his body as he spoke, "Years, I guess."

"Yeah, I can't believe what happen to him. It just ain't a safe old world anymore."

"That's where my job comes in," Parker replied.

"Speakin' of, ya got any idea what went on?" Orin eased down on the couch and propped his feet back on the coffee table.

"Not really. Frank told us he forgot to check on something, and when he went back in, someone hit him from behind." Parker squatted down beside him. "So how's the wound?"

A raw burning ache continued. "Oh, not too bad. The nurse left a while ago. She redressed the bandage."

"Hmm, she might need to come back—looks like there's some seepage."

Frank glanced at a crimson stain where Orin had gripped it.

"We can't have you getting an infection, now can we?"

Through indiscreet shallow breaths, Frank bolstered more poise. "Thanks, I'll have to call them. I'm glad you noticed."

"Sorry, I don't believe I ever caught your name." Parker stood, placed a hand on his hip, eyes riveted on the other man.

"Oh yeah, I'm Billy … Billy Jones. See, me and Frank here, we're distant cousins, third I think. Ain't that right?"

"I never could keep up with all my cousins." Frank's face was rigid as stone.

The portable, police radio squawked.

"Cousins, huh? Excuse me. Gotta check back in. It's a busy day. Well, Mr. Jones, since you arrived by taxi, do you need a ride to the bus station? Or is the plan to stay a few days to care for your cousin?"

"Heck, call me Billy, and I'm not staying, better head back to Georgia." Orin stood and poked his shirttail in his jeans. "Say, it'd be swell if you could take me to the bus depot. I mean, if it ain't no inconvenience. Never rode in a cop car before."

"My pleasure. We don't need to let this old guy get too tired." Parker stuck out a hand. "Frank, take care of yourself, okay? Ready to go, Billy?" He gestured toward the door.

"I'll call ya some time, cuz." The evil grin revealed a broken tooth.

When the door shut, Frank slumped in the recliner, tears in his eyes. *I haven't been so scared since the night they arrested me ... and Orin was the crux of that problem, too. Dear Lord, thank you for Parker.*

He pushed himself up and out of the recliner. Shaky legs led him down the hall to the back door. The dead bolt snapped locked. "Oh no! My .357 Magnum is still at the Short Cut."

The old, arthritic knee impeded a quick return to the front of the house. Shaking, he settled into the recliner, took the remote, and turned the television back on.

The scene flickered, and then a man in a brown suit spoke, "Hello, this is Derek Mosby from Channel 2 Newsroom. We go now to our roving reporter, Kacy Kane."

"Thanks, Derek. I'm here at the Short Cut Bar and Grill." A tall redhead pointed to the front of the building.

Frank's pulse quickened. "What?"

"As you can see, the Griffin County forensic team is still on the scene and hard at work. Over a week ago, the owner, Frank Gunnison, was mugged and shot as he attempted to leave for the night. This establishment has been here for a long time, and Mr. Gunnison is well known and liked. We understand he was recently released from the hospital, but the details are still sketchy. I hope I will have more to report on this unbelievable situation after we receive the results from the crime lab. Back to you, Derek," she concluded.

The remote fell to the floor.

CHAPTER TEN

A relentless, rapid knock on the hotel door shattered Terri's peaceful sleep. "Who is it?"

"Housekeeping," a woman shouted.

Terri rolled over and blinked. The red digital numbers of the small plastic clock displayed 11:15 AM. Heavy covers flew back, and she sat up against the headboard. *Did I forget to set it?*

Tiny slivers of sunlight played peek-a-boo around the edges of the drapes.

"What time is check out?"

"Noon," came the reply.

"Thanks. I'll be gone by then."

Dreamy thoughts from the night before flooded in. A world of strangers glimpsed a different facet of Terri's personality. The applause from the crowd, the clamor for attention, and the line for an autograph, stirred a sense of gratification. A giggle escaped. *Good morning, Lou. Did you sleep well? Yes, yes I did. Thank you very much. And Miss Lou? Yes? Is that a stage name or your real name? Honey, you can't ask a lady to divulge such information. A girl has to have a few secrets, don't cha know.*

At the bathroom sink, a splash of cold water brought new energy. The mirror reflected ebony eyes and raven hair, the uncanny resemblance of Mom. An unexpected relationship materialized last night, yet it baffled Terri. She grew up without a mother. Period. Now, as an adult, it made even less sense. *If a woman falls out of love, okay, but why leave your only child? How does someone's heart grow so cold?*

A ripple of queasiness formed. Arms braced on the sides of the lavatory, Terri buried her head in the oval sink. *It was a one-time act. Lou is gone. Don't want to get close to Mom ... or Loretta ... or whatever she calls herself.* "Frank and the guys at work are my family. My mother's name was Loretta, big deal. It's common. Do you want to Google it?" She spoke to the mirror.

Growing up, there were no pictures of her mother in the house. The one time she asked why, her daddy said, "We simply don't need them. No one can ever love my little girl as much as I do."

End of story.

At the age of four, Chuck took Terri to a nearby zoo. They watched a baby giraffe struggle on lanky legs while the parents stood vigil. The female nuzzled the tiny animal as it continued to labor to stand alone.

"Why didn't Mommy stay and love me? Am I ugly?"

"Oh no, sweetheart, you are beautiful." He replied. "I believe Mommy did love you, but she ... well, she chose to leave."

Dubbed 'Chuck,' Charles Terrance Neal was a tree trunk of a man. Standing 6 foot 5 inches, he had dark curly hair and pale blue eyes. His premature death brought overwhelming grief. Years later, blather from rumormongers still haunted Terri.

After the memorial service, she sent everyone away. Against Frank's protest, the plea to be left alone was finally accepted. Sitting on Chuck's bed, Terri pulled out the nightstand drawer and found a small oak box with brass flower inlay. Inside were several items. One was a black and white picture of a beautiful young woman. It had been crumpled yet straightened out again. Creases striped the photo like a grid. *Maybe the real cause of Daddy's death was a broken heart.*

Next to the photo lay a silver necklace. At the end of the chain, half of a heart dangled. If the other half were attached, it gave the appearance, a verse would be visible. The amulet read, **My Love I Give**.

The blast of a car horn outside dissolved the old reverie. Toothpaste missed the toothbrush and squirted into the sink. *Crap.* Within minutes, she finished, grabbed the toiletries, and slid into a pair of jeans and tee shirt.

Suitcase packed, she started for the door, but stopped. Last night, she left Mom, Weston, and Wade in the café and thanked them for a great time. For a moment, Wade gave the impression he might ask for a phone number. *What would I have said? Oh, Lou doesn't have a cell phone, or a home phone, or even a home, for that matter. I made her up, just like I did as a little girl when I wanted a playmate ... someone like my mommy.*

The hotel door slammed shut, and quick steps led to the car. The Mustang started with a muffled growl. She pulled down the visor to apply some cherry lip-gloss, but a tap on the driver side window made her jump.

A cowboy hat and familiar square face stared back.

"Wade? Where, I mean, how did you find me? What're you doing here?"

"Actually, last night I wanted to talk to you alone. I got up to get Mom more cream for her umpteenth cup of coffee, but when I got back, you were gone. So, I did what any red-blooded cowboy would do—followed the beautiful lady to her car ... and then the hotel."

"You waited, all night?"

"Yup. Slept like a baby in the ol' dually parked next to your pony."

The tenderness in his voice caught her off guard. "Exactly what is your next move, or have you thought that far ahead?" A smile played at the corners of her mouth.

Eyes squinted; a tanned hand rubbed the five o'clock shadow on his jaw. "Well let's see. We've already gone to breakfast. Can't do that. It's pretty close to noon, so I could offer to buy lunch. Seeing as how you stayed in a hotel tells me you live out of town, not to mention the Alabama plates instead of Georgia." He paused. "By all calculations, to ask for a phone number should be the next step in my impromptu plan." He leaned against the truck, legs crossed, and hands in the jean pockets.

The leisure insistent attitude was enticing. Lou seemed to whisper, *"What do we do now?"* A click of the key, and the engine turned off. "Tell ya what. Give me your number, and I'll call you, okay?"

"Maybe not."

"Maybe not, what?"

"If you're married, engaged, or promised to someone, I'm not interested." Wade cocked his head, stance rigid.

"I promise. I'm not any of the above. My job is stressful. I just needed a weekend away."

"Stressful job, huh. What do you do?"

"Well, I'm expected to constantly put out a lot of little fires. Time away energized me. Nothing more."

He reached inside a tooled wallet and squatted beside the open window. "Here's one of my cards for the band. Cell number is in red." Arms on the window ledge, a boyish grin appeared. "When are you coming back to Skirts and Spurs?"

Terri leaned in close enough to feel his breath. A soft hand turned the rough cheek to one side, and her lips brushed it. "Lou never kisses and tells. When I call, it will be a surprise." The engine roared to a start, and dust followed behind as she waved his card out the window.

Taste of Fire
CHAPTER ELEVEN

Two large, red capsules rolled around in Frank's palm like a pair of dice. The medicine regime was a nuisance, but tomorrow the nurse would return and count the number in each bottle. "These suckers are so dang big. Guess this is what you call horse pills." Reluctantly, he popped them in his mouth, took a huge swallow of water, and prayed they didn't lodge in his throat. *I could choke and die trying to get well.* A huge belch followed. *Good grief.* The bedsprings squeaked as he settled under the covers. *I'm so tired ... gotta get some sleep.* The unwanted ring of the phone delayed the chance of rest. He scrambled to reach it. "Hello?"

"Listen, you old bastard, don't hang up," a gruff voice rattled.

Sheer fright loomed. *Orin Chambers.* "Hey, where are you?"

"Your good cop buddy loaned me enough dough for a bus ticket outta town. I pocketed it and hitchhiked to the next county."

"Okay. What're your plans?" Fear hung in his throat.

"Why? Think you're rid of me? Ha! I'll lay low for a while, but there's still the matter of some insurance."

Frank swallowed hard. "Insurance?"

"Don't act stupid, you idiot. I need funds, and I ain't gonna get a frickin' job. You'll provide it or …"

"Or what, Orin?" The threat barbed to the core of Frank's soul.

"Better watch your mouth 'cause I hold all the cards. Next time, my aim will be dead straight," the raspy voice elevated.

"Sorry, sorry, the meds make me jittery. What do you want me to do?" *I have to play his game.*

"I figure you can get one of those round-bottomed nurse friends to run an errand. Wire a thousand bucks to the Western Union in Pell City. Send it under the name of Billy Jones. Remember ol' Billy, your long lost cuz?" A malevolent laugh cackled.

"I've got a little in savings, but not much. I depend on the Short Cut for my living, and as you know, the place is closed."

"Hell, steal it for all I care, but it better reach me by the end of the week … if you don't want another appearance from *Cousin Billy*. Better yet, I can always go visit your darlin', Terri Neal."

Nerves pitched in his stomach. *My God, I have to protect Little T.*

"I also know she's outta town." Orin coughed hard into the phone. "Man, I gotta get me some more cigs. I'm all out."

Frank fought the urge to gag as he listened to the caller hack and spit. "How, how do you know she's gone?

"Don't think I'm not keepin' tabs. I figure she'll come runnin' to your side soon as she gets back. For some idiotic reason, the dumb broad likes ya. It ain't crap to me, but if you don't want her to get pulled into the picture then scrape up the dough."

Click.

The phone shook in a trembling hand until the dial tone went to a steady beep. Sweat dampened the linens. Just a few days ago, life was almost humdrum, now … a crap sandwich.

Inching out of bed, Frank hobbled to the kitchen. Above the refrigerator was a small locked cabinet.

Braced against the counter, he reflected. Yeah, he owned the bar, but he didn't drink the juice, at least not for many years now. Tonight, he needed something to take away the trepidation twisting in his gut. The metal stepstool scrapped as it drug across the linoleum floor. Slow and easy, up one step at a time. On top of the icebox lay a silver key. Anxious fingers unlocked the cabinet to reveal an unopened bottle of Jack Daniels.

The jangle of the phone abruptly intervened—one ring, two, three. An outstretched hand strained for the kitchen phone. *Why did I cheap out and not get caller ID? Gotta answer, even if it is that creep. It'll be worse if I don't.* "Hello?"

"Frank? Did I wake you?"

The sweet sound of Terri's voice brought a semblance of serenity. "Oh no, I'm just a bit slow, but better."

"You sound tired. Are you ready for bed? Do you need anything? I'm back in town and can easily swing by."

Frank closed the cabinet door and stepped off the stool. "No thanks. I took my medicine, and I'm headed to bed. You need to go home and get ready for the week ahead. We'll talk later."

"Are you sure?"

"Yep, but promise me one thing." Thoughts of the previous conversation bubbled.

"Sure," she replied.

"Please check the house good, okay? Have you got a flashlight in the car?"

"Check for what, Frank?"

"Don't open the door to strangers, read the caller ID on the phone, and leave a light on, too."

Taste of Fire

"Has something happened while I was gone? Do I need to come over there?"

"No, nothing happened, but the fact they haven't caught the guy who attacked me is a big concern. Still got a pistol in the car?"

"Yes, I do. Would you feel better if I took it in the house?"

Frank glanced back at the locked cabinet. "Yeah sweetheart, it'd make this old man sleep a lot sounder, and God knows I need it."

◆◆◆◆

An open glove box revealed a .38 snub-nosed Detective Special. Pink polished nails wrapped around the handle, one on the trigger. Thoughts of the perfect score in hand gun class brought an air of confidence. Although reasonable, the seriousness in Frank's voice disturbed Terri. Maybe the recent events, or even the medication, prompted the insistence for safety. Either way, it couldn't hurt to be cautious. His adamant attitude made sense, at least until they solved the case. *I need to stay aware, be observant.*

The motion light flickered on as she approached the porch. Gun down to the side, and purse on one shoulder, she unlocked the door and let it open halfway. Set on a variable timer, the lights inside gave the appearance someone was home ... something her daddy practiced. *If a prowler is stupid enough to break in, I won't hesitate to shoot, that's for sure.*

Content things were safe, she returned to the car for the suitcase. An eye caught Wade's card tucked inside the visor. A silhouette of a guy in a cowboy hat leaned against a guitar. In script read, *Mama's Boys*. Under the group name was *Wade and Weston Carter* and two cell phone numbers. *Wade is definitely easy on the eyes ... but so is Tucker Abraham.*

Taste of Fire
CHAPTER TWELVE

Idle conversation buzzed in Station House Six. Terri sat cross-legged in an overstuffed chair, laptop open, and tried to ignore all the commotion. In the game room, the sports channel blared on the television and cheers rallied. The sweet aroma of blueberry pancakes and bacon wafted from the kitchen as designated cooks took their turn with a skillet and spatula. Howls and hoorahs came from the recreation room as pool balls thudded into the table pockets.

Above it all, the bass voice of Chief McRae boomed over the intercom, "Firefighter Neal, report to my office please. Neal, report to my office."

Like in grade school, one jokester quipped, "Uh-oh. You're in trouble." Another voice sing-songed, "Terri has to go to the principal's office."

She shut the computer, flipped them off, and walked away with a 'red carpet' hip swing.

Inside the private office, a thin faced woman in a prim black suit and white blouse chewed on a fingernail. Coffee-colored hair swept up high and little red glasses on the tip of her nose gave the appearance of a librarian.

"You called for me, Chief?"

"I did. This young woman asked to see you."

The girl stood. "Are you Terri Anne Neal?"

"Yes I am. Who are you?"

"My name isn't important. I am with Peters, Imes, Masterson, and Peters. This is a subpoena." The folded paper shook in her outstretched hand.

Peters, Imes, Masterson, and Peters. Terri envisioned the first letter of each law partner's name, P-I-M-P, and cleared her throat to stifle a giggle. Without emotion, she took the document and read it.

Chief McRae sat behind the desk, hands folded with an expression of surprise on his face.

The young woman turned to him, nodded, and started for the door.

"Whoa, wait. What's this all about, Ms. Peters, Imes, Masterson, and Peters?" A fast step in front of the girl put the two women face to face. "You can't hand me a subpoena and walk away without an explanation,"

"Uh, I'm a legal assistant; actually a temp ... legal assistant. My 90-day probation is up next week. Anyway, I'm not supposed to have to explain anything just deliver the paper to a Ms. Neal. You accepted it, and so it's considered served," the girl's nasal voice wavered.

One hand on a hip, Terri replied, "Honey, I understand, but it's only good manners to tell me. Don't you agree?"

"Well, yes—yes I suppose that's true." A quizzical look appeared.

"Please have a seat." Terri pointed to a chair.

"Oh, no thank you. There are other assignments on my schedule. I represent the law firm of Peters, Imes, Masterson, and Peters." Her shoulders slumped. "Guess I already told you though."

Terri took the girl's hand. "Look, it's obvious you're an intelligent person who wants to make a good impression." She glanced toward the desk. "See, I try to keep my task-master Chief over there happy at my job, too."

The girl's drab green eyes widened.

"You can talk free and confidential in this office. He's a great boss and very understanding. The sooner you explain this little quandary, the quicker you can leave for your next client. Have a seat, and by the way, what's your name again?"

"Oh, I'm Libby, Libby Peters. My Uncle Don owns the firm and ... anyway, our client is Partners Fidelity Insurance Company. The parents of Cilla Wisner, killed in a recent wreck, uh, Cilla, not her parents, well, they decided to sue our client for payment. Since this unit worked the wreck, you in particular, Miss Neal, a summons is necessary for an upcoming court hearing in the matter." The girl paused and let out a big breath. "Wow, it's good to get that off my chest. I hate to deliver bad news."

"Well, there's no other information to offer." Terri pulled a chair parallel in front of Libby's. "Miss Wisner asked me to ride to the hospital in the ambulance. It's not what I usually do, but on this occasion, I agreed. Perhaps she knew death was imminent and didn't want to be alone. Regardless, I did the only humane thing possible at the time."

"Can you remember if Ms. Wisner said anything weird or important before you got to the hospital since she asked for you?" Libby opened a portfolio and took out a steno pad, poised ready to write.

"Firefighters, police, and emergency personnel are civil servants. The title might appear plain, but you have to have heart to perform the job. There was nothing weird. Sad maybe, but not *weird*. What should I have told her? Sorry, I can't go 'cause I gotta get back and wash my fire truck? No, I climbed into the ambulance, held her hand, and silently prayed God would spare this life. Don't you understand? She had extensive burns and internal injuries. The rancid stench of decaying flesh filled the ambulance. I wanted to vomit. Instead, I told her fight to live!"

The pen fell from Libby's hand.

"What does your firm think—this girl divulged some sort of plot to rip off an insurance company? But wait, she forgot she wasn't going to live. Gosh, guess that foiled the strategy a bit, right?" Terri leaned over, inches away from the girl's face.

"No, no ma'am, I mean … did she say that?"

"Are you a crazy idiot?" A rush of adrenaline fueled the words and hands flew upward. "For God's sake, she begged me to not let her die!"

Libby jumped up and grabbed the portfolio. "Thank you both for your time." She pushed the glasses upon her nose and scurried out like a squirrel chased by a barking dog.

Terri crumbled in the chair, the document over her face.

"You did good," the Chief said.

"I did good to ride in the ambulance, or I did good not to slap the snot out of the whiney, little mouse before she escaped in a blur?" Eyes peered over the edge of the paper.

He stared back, stone-faced for a moment, then broke into a guffaw. "I'm sorry, but it was like I could read your thoughts when she rambled off the names of those attorneys." He wiped a laughter tear from his eye.

"Sorry I got so wound up." A half-grin appeared. "Do you think they have a clue how intimidated that moron is just to deliver a silly piece of paper, not to mention the naïveté? I shudder to think if she has to direct interrogatories, take a deposition, or prepare voir dire in court. She'll have a coronary."

TASTE OF FIRE

The Chief shook his head. "I'm afraid you're right."

"So, now the stupid insurance company has hired a PIMP, if you will, to try and keep a dead girl's family from reimbursement on premiums they probably paid for years." She slapped the arm of the chair. "It just is not fair, sir."

"Life isn't fair." He walked around to the front of the desk. "Show up for court, explain what is documented in the report, and let it go. You worked the wreck like a pro and did everything possible to save a life."

"Did I?" She shrugged.

"We both know it was already a code red upon arrival." He leaned back on the edge of the desk, arms crossed. "Don't carry this burden, okay? It is not yours to bear."

◆◆◆◆

The persistent patter of raindrops against the windowpane made it hard for Terri to want to get out of bed. The clock read 5:58 AM. In two minutes, the maddening beep of the alarm would blast into the peaceful softness of a new day. *No more beauty sleep.* She clicked the button to avoid the inevitable. The court appearance for the Cilla Wisner case loomed. *How appropo — overcast and dreary like the whole circumstances of the situation.*

Terri slid off the bed and padded barefoot across the hardwood floor. The coolness of the boards soothed the irritation of her mood toward the day. Under the shower spray, hot water pummeled tight shoulder muscles. Flashes of the horrendous fire and Cilla's screams played over and over. *You should have lived, Cilla. I'm so sorry. Don't worry, I won't give some contemptuous insurance company one iota to enhance their nefarious scheme.*

An early morning rain shower this time of year in Alabama usually meant the welcome sign of spring. Today, it only brought irritation. Keys in hand, she locked the front door.

Vehicles filled every parking space around the Griffin County Courthouse. A block away, Terri squeezed the work jeep next to a dually parked over the yellow stripe. *Jerk.*

A spear of lightning zigzagged across the sky followed by vociferous thunder. The constant sprinkle instantly turned into a colossal downpour.

She grabbed a red umbrella from under the seat. When it refused to open, curse words tumbled like the raindrops.

"Here, let's share mine," a man in a tan overcoat replied.

"Thank you so much." Grateful for the shelter, she ducked under. A familiar face smiled back. "Tucker? What are you doing here?"

"I suppose the same reason you are—the Wisner case." He held the umbrella over them with one hand and slid an arm around her waist.

The warmth of his body made her relax.

Dodging puddles, the couple ran down the sidewalk and up the steps of the building. Under the eave, they turned to face one another. The same magnetism like the first night she met him tickled the pit of her stomach. *Butterflies?*

Down the spacious hallway of the courthouse, pictures of past and present judges lined the corridor in ornate, gold frames. Slick granite walls added a rich contrast. City and county officers mingled while people lingered, engaged in conversation, or hurried along. A small crowd with yellow jury cards in hand waited to one side. Like ants at a picnic, the row of prospective jurors moved toward a table where court clerks checked off names. A mosaic of expressions colored their faces. Terri and Tucker joined the line.

With the dreaded subpoena unfolded, she showed it to a clerk who pointed toward a pair of double doors.

"Do you have to appear in court a lot?"

"I have on occasion." Tucker followed Terri.

"Did a thin, properly dressed, meek paralegal serve you?"

"You described the woman to a tee."

They laughed and started for the security scanner.

Terri's phone rang, and in precision time, Tucker's pager beeped. In unison they said, "It's Frank."

CHAPTER THIRTEEN

A worn handkerchief gently traced the face of the old timepiece. The constant tick matched the patter of rain outside. "Shouldn't be long, now." The watch snapped shut. Frank slipped it in the left trouser pocket and pulled back the sheer from the picture window. Two familiar vehicles pulled into the driveway. "Perfect." The rapid knock was expected.

Terri and Tucker stood on the steps engaged in animated conversation.

"Wanna come in out of the rain, or did ya'll bring some water wings?"

"Egad, I hate this weather." Terri scurried past Frank.

"Thanks." Tucker closed the umbrella, shook off the excess water, and stepped inside.

"You're in serious trouble." Several pillows tumbled to the end of the sofa, and Terri plopped down.

Tucker secured Frank's arm to aid the older man into the recliner.

"Me? Trouble? Don't know what you're jabbering about."

"Mind if I sit down beside you?" Tucker gestured.

"Please do." A hand patted the next cushion. "You texted me and paged Tucker."

Frank tilted his head. "How do you know *I* paged this man, Miss Prissy Pants?"

"Because we were both at the courthouse."

"Funny place to go for a date if you ask me. Doc, do you need a little romantic advice?"

"Frank Gunnison—what's gotten into you? I, I'm sorry, Tucker." A slight blush rushed to her cheeks.

"Courthouse, huh? Wait ... did you go see the Justice of the Peace? Now, that's the kind of news to make an old man get well quick." Frank took a sip of coffee. "There's a fresh pot in the kitchen if anyone's interested."

"Don't change the subject, and stop these silly games," Terri replied.

"Then what were ya'll doing at the courthouse?" The cup rattled in the saucer.

"For crying out loud—remember the girl who died in the car crash, Cilla Wisner? The insurance company refuses to settle with the parents. They subpoenaed us because I worked the wreck and rode to the hospital with her, and Tucker attended in the emergency room."

"So, just when did he become *Tucker* and not Dr. Abraham any more, young lady?"

The couple exchanged glances.

"If it is any of your business, we've been on a first name basis since you were hospitalized. Besides, what's the emergency here? Everything appears okay except your incessant nosiness."

"No emergency." Frank batted his eyes.

"The text said 'Frank's house now'. It terrified me, not to mention I left a very important court case. Are you senile?" She started to get up.

"Wait, Terri." Tucker's hand rested on her forearm. "I have to agree, Frank. Why did you page *me*?"

"Geez, I didn't mean to stir up a hornet's nest. Calm down, Little T, and let me explain."

"Little T?" A smile broke on Tucker's face.

"Never mind, it's a nickname. I'm miffed right now, so this better be good, Frank Gunnison." Terri settled next to the doctor.

Taste of Fire

"Well, a while back I started a conversation with you at the Short Cut, but didn't get to finish." The footrest lowered on the recliner. "I said there was someone I wanted you to meet, someone who came in for a sandwich several times a week. Remember?"

A quizzical look formed. "Sorta."

"Since he was new in town, I asked Doc if he wanted to make some friends. Do you remember?"

"Yes, as a matter of fact, I do," Tucker replied.

"Well, I was talking about the two of *you*."

They faced each other again.

"Him?"

"Her?"

An unusual silence followed.

"This is the deal, kids." He pushed up from the leather chair. "Terri, this here is Dr. Tucker Abraham. He works at Griffin County Hospital and comes in the Short Cut ever so often. We've talked some, but I got a real good feeling about the guy. First off, he loves his work, helping people, saving lives. I asked if he was single, and he said yes. 'Course I wanted to know why, being a professional, and all ... said he just never found the right gal. So, I offered to help the guy out. After all, ain't cha supposed to make new folks in the community feel welcome?"

Terri shook her head. "Frank, I don't ..."

"Now shush, and don't interrupt 'til I'm through, okay?" A finger pressed against his lips.

"Doc also said he hadn't given up hope in the quest for a girlfriend. Next, I asked him if he'd let me find someone to go on sort of a blind date thingy. He was courteous about it, though he might have been just trying to appease an old codger who sells hamburgers and fries. However, he agreed to my idea. Didn't you, Doc?"

"That's exactly right, Frank. By the way, I agreed to the offer because I have respect for you. Heck, any one who can flip burgers and not give me indigestion can't be too far off base." Tucker's eyes were on Terri.

"So Tucker, this is Terri Neal. She's a firefighter and a spirited one, which you probably already figured out. She's got a big heart and loves helping people, saving lives like you. She claims it was her dream as a little girl, but it ain't the truth. Regardless, I'll let her explain that one further. Anyway, she's single." He patted her knee. "For some stupid reason, she cares about the geezer who owns the Short Cut Bar and Grill. Comes in all the time, and ain't above giving marching orders, especially if I'm all banged up like I am right now."

Frank paused and took another sip of coffee. "Okay, all the formal introductions are done. So, please make a grumpy old man happy and go on a date together. You might be right for one another, and you might not, but a date is the first step to find out. Tell me, what's the word?" Frank stood, looking back and forth at the couple.

A big smile formed as Tucker took her hand. "Ms. Neal, I've wanted to go out with you from the first night we met. You turned me down for a cup of coffee, but it didn't bruise my ego. I knew you were emotionally drained from the trauma of the night. However, I made myself a little promise to find you and try again. I did tell Frank I'd be his guinea pig and go on a blind date, but he never told me with whom. I guess I just knew he had good taste. So, I'd love to have the pleasure of your company if you'd say yes."

TASTE OF FIRE

Terri hesitated for a moment as she looked at Frank and then back at the courteous gentleman. "Dr Abraham, *Tucker*, I would love to go out with you." She grinned then cast a small frown at Frank. "Especially since this scoundrel insists on being a matchmaker.

"Well finally." Frank sighed and sat down. "Now, what day and where're you going?"

"Frank," Terri scolded.

"What? Hey, everybody keeps tellin' me I need rest and this took a bunch of energy to finagle. I want to know when the date is, plus how it goes, to boot."

Taste of Fire
CHAPTER FOURTEEN

"Need some help?" Parker Green watched two fellow officers wrangle a handcuffed man through the back entrance of the police department.

"No thanks, Sarge. Got it under control. We're headed to the booking station." The mustached cop tightened the cuffs one more notch.

Sirens blared from another cruiser through the open door.

The dispatcher looked up over the triad of computers she commanded and nodded.

"Hey, Donna, I see Grimes and Cain brought in old man Frey. It must be close to the third of the month, right?" He chuckled.

"Heavens, yes. I've only been here a few months, but already figured out that old buzzard lands in jail every time a social security check arrives. He drinks it up and then wants to fight. Today, Nancy Moore called from the Silver Oaks Nursing Home. She said Clancy Frey was screaming at the top of his lungs he'd take on anybody that wanted to fight and their walker, too." The heavyset, black girl laughed.

"Wait until him and his brother Clarence get into it, girl. We dubbed them 'Rough and Ready'. Clarence lives one town over and sometimes hitchhikes to Anniston. We stay prepared to arrest the dynamic duo because inevitably it happens. They sleep it off and get a couple of free meals out of the deal. When they go before the Municipal Court judge, both promise never to do it again—same old worn out excuse. I think Judge Summers gets a kick out of them, or else she'd already put a stop to their shenanigans."

Taste of Fire

The radio blared, "Dispatch, I need a 10-27." Donna shook her head. "Gotta run a drivers license check for King."

Down the hallway, Parker entered the criminal investigation department. Two men and a woman sat behind desks, files and papers stacked high.

"Any of the forensic guys back there?" He pointed toward the lab area.

"As a matter of fact, Nguyen asked about you a little earlier," one detective replied.

"Thanks." He headed toward the double metal doors. "Jon, I heard you were looking for me."

A young Vietnamese man in a stained, white lab coat met his gaze. "Yes, I wanted to show you something unusual." He pulled out a glass slide from a microscope and placed it in a tray. "We got something from the crime scene at the Short Cut Bar and Grill. You said the owner is a friend of yours, and I thought it might help expedite the investigation."

"Great, what is it?"

The stool rolled backward as he walked to a file cabinet. "Actually, it's a photo of a boot print found at the entrance to the building." Against an illuminated screen, Jon attached the snapshot.

"Look, I know you're the expert, but that's a high traffic area. What makes this one special?"

"Granted, there is a variety of shoes and boots, and under ordinary circumstances it might have gone undetected. However, a group of colleagues and I recently attended a two-week training session at a school in Birmingham where they discussed this very issue. I ascertained new information and procedures to detect miniscule differences. The pattern of wear, the size, the shape, even the heel or toe force as a person bears down when they …"

"Okay, okay I understand the intricacy, but what's the deal on this particular print?"

"I realize your impatience, although I don't appreciate it." The picture popped as Jon jerked it from the screen.

"Hey man, didn't mean to sound rude. Sorry, but I don't have time to go through your interpretation of the course before we figure out who'd have the audacity to hurt Frank Gunnison. You've been to the Short Cut. He's a good guy; much like yourself."

"Comparatively speaking it's very small for a man … at least if you are not of my decent." Jon gave a conservative smile.

"So, how can you tell it isn't someone Asian, or oriental, or whatever?"

"Honestly, I cannot, but I do have access to this magnificent machine." He gestured to a flat screen. "CID let us buy the high-tech software sold at the conference. The new program provides an advanced database that gives variables to narrow the search. I felt confident before I entered the data, but did so to validate my conclusion. The pattern we see is unique only because this shoe isn't available at any of the regular camping stores or discount warehouses."

The lab door swung open, and a lanky, bald-headed man entered. "Hey Parker, I see you got the picture of the boot print. Wow, what an easy answer."

A finger quickly went up to Nguyen's lips in protest.

Parker glanced from one man to the other. "Uh, easy you say? Well Blake, why don't *you* tell me?"

"Thanks, big blabbermouth." Jon scowled. "Blabbermouth Blake … that's what your new nickname is from now on." The forensic specialist crossed his arms. "Okay, okay. What I didn't have *time* to say is … this print style happened to be one of the examples we were given at the school."

He retrieved a notebook from the shelf and flipped through pages of notes and pictures. After a finger stopped on a black and white photo, Jon walked to the copier and ran a print. "See this is very, very similar to what we extracted. The sweet clue here is it is a military issued shoe only available at a BX or in a military base environment. Other than that, we are still working on all the fingerprints found and running each through CODUS. If we get any hits, I will definitely let you know. Hope this helps."

"Can I have this?" Before a reply came, Parker headed for his patrol car, photo in hand.

CHAPTER FIFTEEN

Danielle slowly pulled the corner of the soiled bandage from Frank's shoulder. "The wound looks very good, Mr. Gunnison. There does not appear to be any more seepage, only a dab of blood here in a couple small spots. I can see the skin starting to produce a scab around the opening, which means it needs air in order to heal quicker. In addition, there's less swelling. I'm going to minimize the dressing for better mobility and allow more freedom in your range of motion."

Frank relaxed as the coolness of her fingers worked on the injured area.

"The size of the knot on your head is smaller, and the contusion is a nice yellowy-green color—an indication there isn't any clotting to worry about. All in all, we can document a much improved report today."

A hint of perfume filled his nostrils while she went about the routine checkup. He closed his eyes. *If I look, all I see are ample breasts. I ain't dead, thank the good Lord, but I ain't no spry, young chicken, either. Better keep my peepers shut.*

"I'm all through now, Mr. Gunnison. Open your eyes. Hope it wasn't too painful."

"Thanks, little lady. I appreciate the kindness and wonderful care."

"You're one of my favorite patients. I'm just glad I can help." The young nurse patted his hand.

"Could you do something else for me?"

Danielle slipped the stained materials in a hazardous waste bag and zipped it shut. "Sure, Mr. Gunnison."

"Please, tell those folks at Meals to Go I can fix my own food. They don't need to come by any more." Frank buttoned up his shirt.

"Are you sure? Dr. Abraham gave us strict orders, and he hasn't made any changes."

"Yes ma'am. Besides, I'll never get the soreness out if I don't move around some. All strapped down by them dang bandages made me feel like it was glued to my side. Now, I can do more."

"Let me talk to my supervisor first." Supplies put away, she headed out. "I'll be back to check on you. Have a good day."

A wave to the nurse, and Frank secured the lock. "I have to get the Short Cut back in business. No paycheck is killing me, not to mention the damn money Orin made me wire him." The words barely left his lips before the cordless phone rang. "Hello?"

"Yeah, hello *Mr. Banker.*"

The mere sound of the voice prickled the skin on Frank's arms. "Uh, Orin, how are you?"

"Like you give a damn, but I have to say, the little tad of money you sent me did help out."

"Little tad? I consider a thousand dollars a lot of money." The weight of his body fell against the door.

"Oh well, too bad. I done spent it all. So, I need you to send more, and now!"

"Look man, you know I'm laid up. The Short Cut is closed. There's no money coming in. What do you want me to do?"

"Frankly, my dear, I don't give a damn." Gruff laughter filtered through the phone.

"You gotta let me get back on my feet, okay?" He shuffled to the end of the couch and collapsed.

TASTE OF FIRE

"No—wire me the next installment. If I have to make another visit, there'll be a pit stop at *somebody's* house first."

"I'm not even well enough to drive, and the nurse just left," Frank pleaded.

"Send it to the same place as before … tomorrow … by 6:00 PM." A dial tone hummed.

Daylight faded, and shadows in the living room loomed like Halloween figures. Head in his hands, Frank slumped to one side in the depressing darkness. A couple thousand dollars was left in his savings account, but the business required cash to operate, too. Orders needed filling and vendors paid, but tomorrow he'd call Danielle and ask for a favor. How could a stupid, white lie about going to Viet Nam snowball into a full-blown avalanche?

The small pendulum clock on the wall bonged seven chimes.

Eyes now adjusted to the dimness, the inky blackness shrouded Frank like a heavy cloak. *I've never felt so alone.* Relentless frustration produced irrepressible weeping. The spasmodic breathing made his chest burn as though a branding iron held him against the couch. *What evil have I set in motion?*

Taste of Fire
CHAPTER SIXTEEN

Chatter buzzed in the middle bay while swing shift washed and scrubbed Engine Number Five. The crew joked and laughed. Wet mops sloshed across the hood and sides as boots waded through puddles of foamy water.

Hair pulled back in a ponytail, Terri sat on top next to a bucket of suds and sponges. She took a slight breath in, tried to cover her mouth, but a big sneeze blew bubbles everywhere.

"What's up? You always do that when we clean the rigs," a short guy in rubber galoshes quipped.

"You're supposed to say *God bless you*, Hank Rodgers." A soapy sponge flew past his ear. "Maybe I'm allergic to the stupid detergent."

"Are you allergic to this?" a deeper voice replied.

A shot of water blasted upward, and she squealed. "J.R., you're in trouble, now. Good thing this reservoir isn't full. I'd use the water cannon to blast you into tomorrow." Climbing down to retaliate, her cell phone rang. "Wait, wait." She dashed toward the door. "Gotta phone call."

"Sure Neal, likely excuse," someone yelled from the other side of the bay. "You'll get it when you come back though."

"Oh hush, Matt. Besides, you'll have to catch me first." Terri took refuge in the empty recreation room. A puddle of water trailed behind. "Hello, Neal here." Droplets trickled off her forehead.

"Hey, this is Tucker. Did I catch you at a bad time? Sounds like you've been running."

A tingle surged at the sound of his voice. "No, we decided to wash the trucks, and it turned into a water fight. Your call saved me from getting drenched. How's your day going?"

"Whenever I get to hear your voice, it's always a good day. Listen, I wondered if you were free tomorrow night, you know, for our blind date. Can't have Frank in a perpetual uproar."

A tug at the rubber band and damp curls tumbled. "Well, let me ask my social secretary." A giggle escaped. "Yep, looks like I'm open."

"Whew, that's great. I forgot all about the *secretary* thing. How about seven o'clock?"

"Sounds good. How should I dress?" A finger twisted a strand of hair.

"I'll let you pick—casual or dressy, lady's choice."

"Where're we going?"

"You pick the clothes; I'll surprise you with the place."

"Oh, you're a tricky one, but I choose ... dressy."

♦♦♦♦

In front of an ivory painted, antique vanity, Terri sat on a padded bench with a blue towel wrapped around her body. Pale pink roses graced the face of four little side drawers. She let a finger follow the delicate floral design of the lap drawer.

After his wife left, Chuck Neal promptly gave all her belongings to charity except this one piece of furniture. It remained a testament of the woman's artistic talent. He told Terri they bought it at a rummage sale for mere pennies. In need of repair, the couple worked side by side to refinish it before their daughter's birth. Although a bittersweet memory, she was glad now he saved it.

"I suppose there was some good my mother left behind."

TASTE OF FIRE

The hinged mirrors gave a glimpse of three images. She stared at the scar on her arm, and a visual landslide formed—Cilla Wisner's screams for help, the inferno wreckage, and the violent explosion. *I just can't seem to let those images go.*

While on the witness stand, the attorneys took every detail Terri recounted and picked it apart like aggressive buzzards over road kill. Disgust boiled inside, but she never wavered.

Thoughts of Tucker's strong voice, yet velvet-edged, made her proud as he recounted each trained action taken in the emergency room. The explanation sounded like her father talking. The human side of the profession was to save lives, and a noble effort was vehemently attempted. The expression on Tucker's face confirmed the words were chosen carefully to conserve additional angst for the Wisners.

She could empathize. The scar was a daily reminder of her own mortality. *When the car caught on fire, the flame tasted your arm and was afraid. It knew you were special.* Reminded of her father's words, gratitude settled in. *What really made me so different? If I could have gotten to Cilla sooner, maybe the fire would have spared her, too.*

Remorse would never bring back Cilla, much less Terri's mother. Her daddy never indicated his wife should have died in the car fire, but the abandonment felt like a fatality. *How could a mother choose to leave a child unless by death?* She shook her head as if to erase the thoughts of misery and heartache.

Tonight though, tonight was special. Maybe through Cilla's demise, God's plan was to bring new life into Terri's world. Her eyes twinkled in the mirror as the mascara thickened. A tube of Rosy Revelation lined plump lips, and a mist of hair spray filtered through the air.

Coat hangers rattled on the rod while she raked through the closet. "Ah, perfect."

The price tag dangled like a leaf in the wind. One snip of the scissors, and it landed in the trashcan. She wiggled into the ruby red, strapless dress, buckled the wide black belt, and smoothed down the lace-scalloped hem. *Well, I bought this outfit on sale for a special occasion, and I'd say Dr. Tucker Abraham qualifies as very special.*

After slipping on a pair of black heels with rhinestones, she checked the mirror one more time.

"Almost forgot." One hand grabbed a cut-glass decanter of perfume. "Haven't used any of this in a while." The bottle read *Pleasurable Destiny*. A dab went behind each ear lobe and wrist just as the doorbell chimed. After a second thought, she placed a drop between her breasts.

◆◆◆◆

At the front door, a massive arrangement of yellow roses and lavender masked the person behind them.

"Tucker?"

Head tilted to one side, he peeked above the bountiful array, an eyebrow raised. "Flowers for the lady."

"Oh, they're beautiful. I wasn't—I mean. I didn't expect flowers. Please, please come in," Terri fumbled the words. "Let me get a vase. Have a seat, and I'll be right back."

He watched her gently pick each bud and sniff the fragrance before it found a place in the crystal container.

"How'd you know my favorite is yellow roses?"

"There's a lot about you I've learned, but I'll admit my source ... if you can't guess."

"Frank?" Terri smiled.

Dedicated hours and tiresome shifts left little time for a social life. It had been a while since Tucker enjoyed the pleasure of a woman's company. There was an instant attraction to the lady firefighter that first night in the hospital. Those mahogany eyes stirred more than mere concern or admiration. She went the extra mile to comfort a dying young girl. He likened those traits to his own persona, and it didn't hurt the woman was gorgeous, too.

"May I say you look absolutely stunning in that dress?" He walked over to the counter where she busily filled the vase.

"Why Dr. Abraham, thank you very much. I'd like to add, you look very debonair tonight yourself."

"Oh this little thing?" Tucker strutted and turned.

"The black jacket is from 'Days of the Past' along with the slacks. As you can see, I chose a navy blue, Oxford button-down shirt. By the way, if you notice, it sets off my eyes. A light blue and black striped tie completes the outfit." A whirl on one heel, he walked down the hall and out of sight.

Terri's laughter filled the room.

A moment later, he peeked around the corner.

"Is this a spin-off of your bedside manner, or am I the only one privy to it?"

He stepped to her side, fingers warm on her cool arm. In a mutual quiet moment, their eyes locked. Close enough to feel her breath, he memorized every feature; sensual eyes, turned up nose, full red lips. *Oh to taste your kiss, but not now ... patience.*

She opened her mouth as if to speak, but he intervened, "Are you hungry? I'm starved. Better get a move on. We have reservations at La Petite St. Simone's."

CHAPTER SEVENTEEN

In the circular drive of the renowned restaurant, La Petite St. Simones, the headlights of Tucker's SUV flashed across a life-size marble statuary. In its arms, an urn spewed a continuous flow of water into a layered fountain below.

After the valet took the keys, a gloved door attendant walked the couple through the triangular glass foyer.

A small stairway led to an elevator with thick glass walls. The words 'Buon Appetito' were etched on all four sides. On the next floor, the door slid open to reveal an elegant eatery.

"What was inscribed back there?" Terri whispered.

"I believe it said *enjoy the meal*, which will be easy." He smiled.

Terri slid an arm through his. "Why so confident?"

"Because I'm with you."

Inside the restaurant, a five-piece string ensemble serenaded the crowd with soft classical music. A low din of conversation drifted throughout the stylish and chic surroundings.

The maitre'd escorted them to a table for two where a single lit candle surrounded by yellow rose petals sat in the center.

Tucker held the back of the chair and waited on Terri before sitting across from her. "Looks like yellow roses are the flower de jour." He motioned toward the centerpiece.

"Those are nice, but no comparison to mine." An amber glow from the candle brightened her face.

Taste of Fire

He reached over and let his hand rest on hers. "You look beautiful tonight, and I think this is even better."

"Excuse me?"

"The night we met at the hospital, I asked if you wanted to go have a cup of coffee. Glad you turned me down now ... this is much better."

The waiter cleared his throat. "Good evening mademoiselle and monsieur. May I offer you a menu?"

They took a little time to peruse the list.

When the server returned, Tucker said, "Would you care if I order for us?"

"Oh, I'd be delighted." She placed the leather-bound menu on the table

In fluent French, the doctor gave the waiter their selections and ordered an aged bottle of Chardonnay.

Terri crossed her arms. "Impressive—you speak French. Obviously, there's a lot I don't know about you."

"Ah, so you thought I was just a good ol' boy from the South, right?"

"Well, I hadn't thought about it, but please tell me more."

"Only if you return the favor. Fair enough?"

"Okay, but you go first," Terri replied.

"Well, I was born in Atlanta. Early on, my father took off and left Mother with all the parental responsibilities. At that point, I became the man of the house working and going to school to help shoulder the load. Sports provided a full ride scholarship to Georgia Tech ... go Bulldogs," he spoke it low, but like a chant. "My internship was up north, but family is important so I came back home," he added.

"Goodness, I'm even more impressed. Are there any siblings?"

Taste of Fire

"I am the oldest, but I have a couple of sisters. Now, what about you?"

Tucker watched the sparkle in those profound brown eyes fade as she looked down. The expression was reminiscent when he had delivered unpleasant news to a patient or family member. Apparent pain showed on her face.

A finger twisted a long curl. "You know about Frank. He and my father were friends since junior high school. While Frank went off to war, my parents married. Daddy was a Captain for the Griffin County Fire Department when …"

He realized she was visibly shaking and moved his chair closer. An arm encircled her shoulder.

She jumped at the touch. "Most of the time, I'm not a very emotional person, but some things are harder to talk about than others."

"Look, if it's too complicated or arduous to discuss, I understand. What I already know is plenty for me." He turned her cheek toward him and looked into her sad eyes.

"No, I want to talk about this—to you, at least. Obviously, I don't try to hide the scar on my arm." A finger pointed to the marred skin.

"Yes, I saw it. It doesn't bother me. We all have scars. Life does that to us. You have one on the outside, and it shows. Many people have them on the inside and aren't brave enough to admit it."

"You have such compassion, but I guess it's normal in your profession. I must admit, the night we met I felt as though we were old friends, comfortable and at ease near you. Yes, it was a traumatic night, but it's part of my occupation. We both have to deal with the ugliness thrown into innocent people's paths. However, the situation with Cilla Wisner reopened a Pandora's Box of my own past." She took a deep breath.

"My father passed away a couple years ago. Such a gentle giant. It was a horrible shock. He raised me as a single parent, and we were extremely close. I don't know if my mother is alive or dead. As a child, Daddy recalled this story a million times.

"It was a rain slick night when Mommy put you and your toy bear in the car. She was frightened of the weather, but had an important errand to run. She drank some bad medicine earlier that made her lose control and crash into a tree. The car caught on fire, yet when the flame tasted your arm, it was afraid. The fire knew you were special."

Tucker listened as the emotion in Terri's voice rose and fell in pitch. The rage in her eyes spoke the words of fear, sorrow, and anger.

"Years later, I learned the bad medicine he spoke of was whiskey. She left a while after the accident, but I was too young to understand. It never made sense how a mother could abandon a child. I certainly couldn't." The silverware rattled as her hand slapped the table.

He pulled her closer. "Terri, thank you for sharing such private information. We know life isn't fair, but what I see is a beautiful, young woman who has taken those trials and tribulations and grown from it. You do it on a daily basis—every time the fire alarm sounds at work. On goes an armor of determination and you take up the sword of compassion to slay the iniquitous dragons for other people ... most you've never met, nor will again."

A glimmer of a smile appeared, and he watched the softness return to her face.

"That is quite a portrayal, Dr. Abraham. Such insight is very uncanny. Why is it so easy to spill my guts to you? Are you a psychologist, too?"

He let out a hearty laugh. "Maybe I have a good eye for detail."

The waiter appeared with a tray of food.

While they ate and chatted, Tucker sensed an easy calm settled over his blind date. A tender strength glowed, and it captivated him. "Listen, the night air is light and cool. Would you like to go out on the terrace for another glass of wine?"

"Sounds just like what the doctor ordered."

TASTE OF FIRE
CHAPTER EIGHTEEN

The new couple stood side by side on the balcony, alone.

Terri took a deep breath. The musky aroma of cologne brought a heady sensation.

Tiny twinkle lights wrapped around stone columns across the portico flickered like miniature diamonds. Down below, a small pond surrounded by lush ferns gurgled. Lanterns spotlighted the edges casting a radiance of ripples. Light reflected off the water like wheat colored ribbons.

The doctor took a quarter from his pants pocket and tossed it in the air. The coin spiraled downward with a slight splash. "Make a wish."

"What?" Terri said.

"Mine already came true."

"Really?"

A breeze toyed with the fragrance of magnolia blossoms nearby.

She faced Tucker, a hand on each sturdy shoulder and watched his gaze drop to the creamy softness of her bosom. "I'm not a trophy."

"Nor did I ever think you were. However, I do have to say, instead of extinguishing a flame, the lady firefighter ignited one tonight."

"Another feature of your bedside manner?"

"Not to be flippant, but I gave my heart away once."

"Once?"

"Seriously, only once.

"Do you want to talk about it?"

"Let's just say the circumstances weren't right. It didn't work. Afterwards, I vowed to be cautious."

"Don't tell me a social life doesn't exist." Terri rolled her eyes.

"There are friends at work, but no one special. Yet, the moment we met something changed, felt right. I didn't even know if I'd ever see you again. Remember, you turned me down?" He chuckled.

"Was it just luck of the draw Frank became your patient?"

"Luck is the key word, or should I say fate? I was scheduled to be off, but at the last moment traded shifts with a young intern so he could study for a big exam. Don't forget, Frank schemed for us to meet for a good while. Horoscopes and palm readers give me the willies. Still, what do *you* call it?"

Except for the occasional chirp of a katydid, or the bubble from the brook, the question created a sudden hush.

For the first time, Terri wondered about her future. *What is missing? Throughout my life, I never witnessed the mature love of a couple. Could it be?*

Tucker lifted her chin, and his lips found hers.

The initial intimacy sent a blaze and brought an undeniable spark of arousal. She wanted more, needed more, but pushed away.

"Tucker, I ..."

"No. Let me apologize. I was too forward. I'm sorry." He took her hand and led the way to a table where two crystal glasses waited next to an iced bottle of champagne.

"Haven't done this in a very long time. Better watch out for flying objects." The cork popped and landed a few feet away. Bubbles fizzed as he poured. "Can I make a toast?"

"Please do."

Taste of Fire

He lifted his glass. "To Frank."

"To Frank," she echoed.

Their crystal clinked in unison.

◆◆◆◆

Soft rock music played on the car radio, but Terri hated they rode in silence.

In the driveway of the Neal house, Tucker got out and opened her car door.

A strong hand steadied the way as she exited. *Funny how his touch always makes me feel safe.*

The porch light emitted a soft glimmer as they ascended the steps.

Eyes downward, she spoke, "I had a lovely time tonight. Thank you."

"It was definitely my pleasure." He took a step back. "Goodnight."

Before he made it to the sidewalk, she held up a hand. "Wait."

The doctor turned on one heel. "Yes?"

"I, I don't know what to say."

Slowly, he returned to her. "I do. This might be a mistake, but I have to be truthful even if you think it sounds corny. Something magical happened when we met, at least for me. I've tried to put you out of my mind, but fate, or Frank, or something yanked you back. Honesty is paramount. I can't run my life on lies whether in a relationship or the operating room. Perhaps in your eyes, I over stepped a boundary with the kiss tonight, but at least now you know how I feel."

She paused for a moment. "It's a bit chilly out here." The keys jangled in the lock. "Do you want to come inside?" A yellow tabby cat meowed as the door opened.

TASTE OF FIRE

"This is LC, man of the house." Terri picked up the pet.

"Looks like a fine male specimen to me. What do the initials stand for, if you don't mind me asking?"

"He was the last to survive an abandoned litter. All the rest were lunch for a huge snake, perhaps the mother, too. When I rescued the tiny thing, I started calling him LC for *lucky cat*."

"Pretty unique. I like that story." He rubbed the cat's ears, and it let out a low purr.

"Funny, I've never seen him take to a stranger so quick. He's picky—like me." She handed him the cat.

"Mind if I sit down and have a little man-to-man talk with my new buddy?"

Terri swept a hand in the direction of the couch.

The twosome settled between several colorful throw pillows. "This is how it is, LC. By mere chance, I met this awesome woman, the same one who feeds you every day. Since then, I can't seem to concentrate on much else. She might think I'm some sort of goon for laying the cards on the table, but legend says, a real Queen of Hearts only trumps the King once in a lifetime."

The pet circled Tucker's lap and snuggled into the crook of his arm.

"Uh, would you like some coffee or maybe a cup of cocoa? There's also a couple beers in the fridge."

"Some ice water would be great," Tucker replied.

Terri returned with a tall glass of water in hand. As she moved around the coffee table, her heel caught in a braided rug. Ice cubes and water splattered on Tucker and his newfound friend.

The cat screeched, bounded down, and out of sight.

Tucker stood, shirt and coat dripping wet.

TASTE OF FIRE

"Oh gracious, I'm so sorry!" Terri ran to the kitchen for some hand towels, but when she entered the living room, she found Tucker doubled over holding his stomach. "Oh my gosh, are you sick? What's wrong?"

He straightened up and continued laughing. "Uh, I'm fine, but I think LC might be traumatized."

"My stars, I'm so embarrassed. How could I be so clumsy?" She dabbed at the soaked area of the shirt and jacket. "Here, take off those wet things. I'll be right back."

A rumble and thud came from the hall closet as the ironing board fell to the floor. She drug it into the living room. "Now where is the dang iron?"

"Terri, Terri, please come here. It isn't a big deal. Really."

"No, I mean, yes, it is, I ..." She looked up to see a sculpted muscular torso—the shirt, jacket, and tie spread across the back of the couch.

Methodically, he retrieved the ironing board and set it upright. "Accidents happen, but this isn't." Once again, he kissed her.

This time, she molded against him. Raked her fingers through his hair.

He nipped gently at the skin on her neck and kissed the bareness of her shoulders.

They lingered in the embrace as the kisses became more torrid and passionate.

Then, he stopped and held her at arm's length. "Terri."

Without a word, she led him down the hall.

The security light filtered through the beige gossamer curtains and cast a pale beam across the bed. She let a hand linger on his chiseled chest before removing her black belt. Arms behind her, the zipper buzzed, and the red dress fell to the floor.

In a few moments, they stood naked in the soft blackness of the bedroom. Swept up in his arms, he placed her on the bed. She buried her face in the chorded muscles of his neck.

His touch was persuasive and invited more as he rose above her. Gently, his tongue travelled her body like a road map. Hands skimmed past her rib cage down to a flat stomach. He paused and looked up at her face dimly illuminated from the soft outside light. "I can stop, you know."

"Shhh," came the reply.

"Are you sure?"

"Yes," she whispered.

Taste of Fire
CHAPTER NINETEEN

The yellow police tape snapped as Frank traipsed outside the Short Cut Bar and Grill ripping it off. Wadded up in a ball, he tossed the streamer in the trash bin. *Stupid crime scene.* A stiff shoulder, and constant ache in the distressed knee, shadowed any thoughts of a good mood. "Geez, it sucks to get old."

Inside the diner, a sharp odor of cooked onions lingered. He ran a finger across the dusty counter. "Well, I ain't got no maid to clean up. Guess I better use some elbow grease and quit complaining."

A flick of the switch and the neon beer signs flickered and buzzed. Coins rattled in the jukebox as he punched in B3.

George Strait crooned a country tune while Frank filled up the mop bucket. The water sloshed against the sides, and a wave of nausea swelled at the thought of Orin Chambers and the gun. "Seems this old bucket and me got some secrets to keep."

After several grunts and curse words, the dried blood on the floor was gone, the counter clean, and a strong smell of bleach remained.

He eased down on a bar stool and blotted beads of sweat from his forehead with a hand towel. "Bless Little T's heart for making up some flyers. Her and those 'grand re-opening' ideas. Maybe most of the old crowd will straggle in since she got word out I'm open again."

◆◆◆◆

Despite portentous, gray storm clouds, the atmosphere was upbeat at Station House Six. Thunder rumbled like a hungry lion, and soon an army of lightning bolts serrated the sky.

TASTE OF FIRE

"All those reports are filed, Chief," Terri said.

"Thanks Neal, you know I can't keep my file box clear without your help." He chuckled. "Hey, I heard the Short Cut is back in business. Guess ol' Frank is going to live after all, huh?

"Yeah, today is his first day open. I thought I'd go by after shift and lend a hand. He's really been in a bind without any money coming in. I offered to help, but no go—wouldn't even consider a loan."

The fire alarm clanged and interrupted their conversation.

"Duty calls." Terri mocked a salute.

"Yup, better bunk up," Chief replied.

Engine Number Five roared to a start and rolled into traffic with the ladder truck close behind.

At 148 North Claude Street, lightning had struck a tree and sparks ignited the roof of a small frame house nearby. Chunky dark smoke clawed at the sky, and flames raced throughout the fragile structure as help arrived.

In practiced organization, the crews went straight to work. Terri, and two other firefighters, manhandled the hose like a snake charmer as they inched closer and closer to the building.

Several neighbors gathered around an elderly black man, the owner who managed to escape the disaster moments before.

"Please save my cat. Please, please save Gracie. She's all I've got," the old man cried.

"I'll go in after it." Terri checked the oxygen equipment. It was only half-full. *Oh dear Lord, I should have spent more time on maintenance and less in the Chief's office. I know better than to break the rules.*

Taste of Fire

A black velvet curtain of smoke crept up the walls as she entered the smoldering house. Terri kept low, the shield locked down over her face, and eyes wide. *Gotta make this quick, in and out.* A wooden beam crackled, and she crouched as it plunged downward. Two interior walls disintegrated and embers scattered as the charred remains fell only inches away. Flames formed a glaring fury. *Where is Gracie?* A section of the particleboard floor collapsed and one leg went through the opening. *I'm stuck!* Her pulse quickened. After three slow breaths, she regrouped, pushed hard, and forced herself out of the splintered wood. On hands and knees, she stared at what appeared to be the kitchen. Scrunched in a corner sat a gray kitten. Slow and steady, she crawled over and scooped it up. Smoke hovered like a swarm of angry bees.

Iron-willed, she turned to retreat from the holocaust, but the fragile burnt doorframe snapped and brought down a ceiling joist. Sparks danced like glittery red fairies. Spears of fire lashed like a wild bullwhip as the hideous inferno took on the appearance of a starving beast, devouring everything in its path.

With the tiny animal cradled under one arm, she sat frozen, rooted to the spot, and eyes riveted on the scene. *What ... what is that? An image of a face? Daddy?* She saw his smile, heard his voice, and then ... closed her eyes.

"Unbutton that bunker jacket. Take off her helmet. Get an oxygen mask, and hurry!"

Who is screaming? Why am I lying down? Is that rain on my face?

"Neal? Neal? Can you hear me?" Chief McRae hollered.

TASTE OF FIRE

"Yeah, uh, I'm fine. What happened? Who's manning the hose? Geesh, don't we need to get in out of the rain?" A choking cough stung her throat.

"If she can start giving *me* orders, I would say she's gonna be fine." He laughed.

Hank Rodgers and Monte Peterson lifted her to a standing position.

"Thanks guys." She held on to Monte.

"A beam trapped you. We were afraid you took in too much smoke. You were pretty woozy."

"And Gracie?"

"The kitten is fine," the Chief replied. "The gentleman it belongs to sends his gratitude." He patted her on the back. "I had just arrived when several guys went in to find you and the cat. They said you were talking some mumbo jumbo. I was worried you experienced a little trauma," he continued.

"Mumbo jumbo? What do you mean?" She rubbed her leg.

"Couldn't understand everything. Something about dancing with the fire, or dancing with your daddy, or words to that effect."

◆◆◆◆

After shift, Terri headed to the Short Cut. It was imperative to talk to Frank about the likeness of her father's face in the fire. *What an experience. I didn't imagine it ... he spoke my name, took my hands. We did dance ... and talked.* Frank would be the only one to help me make sense of things.

As she rounded the corner to the bar, Frank's brown and tan truck passed going the opposite direction. She threw up a hand and waved, but he flew past, a scowl ensconced on his face. *So unlike him. Besides, he should have recognized my car. There's not another yellow '66 Mustang in town.*

Terri whirled around in the parking lot of a closed down construction company. The tires sent bits of pea gravel sailing through the air as she sped up to follow. *He probably needed to run an errand before Happy Hour starts. When I catch up, maybe we can go for a quick cup of coffee, and I'll tell him what happened.*

A few cars behind, she watched Frank drive past the bank, the supermarket, and two liquor stores. *Where in the devil are you going? Those are all the usual stops.*

The truck ventured into a part of town the cops called 'Rauch'. Known drug dealers traversed the dim lit streets at night, and young girls worked the corners prostituting their bodies for crack, heroin, or a few lousy dollars. The houses all displayed burglar bars, and drive by shooting were a constant problem. Graffiti, in a kaleidoscope of colors, covered the outside walls of every accessible vacant building. *It's creepy and dangerous, Frank. What business do you have over here? You don't belong, and neither do I.*

The familiar old truck parked in front of a sleazy, run-down pawnshop. The sign overhead read 'John's Hometown Hock and Shop'.

Terri eased a foot off the accelerator and circled the block only to see Frank's vehicle still parked there. A knot formed in her stomach. Was she more afraid of him seeing her or the undesirables who might try to hijack her car in broad daylight?

At the second corner down, a glance in the rear view mirror revealed the tan and brown pickup headed north toward town. *Okay girl, common sense says follow him and talk about the image in the fire today.* Memories of the date with Tucker brought a rush. *When did I ever listen to common sense? There has to be some explanation for Frank going in this dumpy joint, and I have to find out why.*

Determined, she locked the car and went inside. Tarnished metal bells on a frayed, dirty string jingled as the door opened. The room smelled stale. Shelves lined the walls with appliances, electronic devices, musical instruments, and miscellaneous junk. Over the main counter hung a mounted elk head, cobwebs dangled on each tine. Straight ahead was a glass partition framed by wrought iron bars. It appeared to be bulletproof with a round opening in the center to speak through and a low square area to exchange money.

A semi-bald man with a bushy mustache approached. The stub of a chewed cigar hung from the corner of his mouth. A greasy tee shirt and red suspenders stretched over a barrel-size belly. "Well, well, well. Hel-lo there. What can ol' honest John do for ya today?" Ashes tumbled as he spoke.

"Honest John, huh?" Terri cocked an eyebrow.

"Yup baby. That's what they call me, but you can call me anything you like, cute as you are." A Cheshire cat smile spread across his face.

Disgusted, she steeled her gaze. "I see. Well, what I need to know, Mr. Honest John is what did the gentleman who just left your business establishment buy?" Lips pursed, she leaned forward.

"My business estab ... uh, what'd you call it? I like fancy words." Halitosis rolled through the circular glass opening.

Terri stifled the urge to gag. "Establishment. That's what you have here—a company, a corporation, a business establishment." Reluctantly, she batted her eyes.

"Yeah. Sure. I knew that. Uh, well he didn't buy anything, but he sure hocked something purdy."

"Might I see the item?"

The smelly owner grabbed something from the glass case below the window.

She recognized it immediately. *Frank's antique pocket watch. His most prized possession.*

"This is the little jewel. Ain't it a beaut?"

"Oh, some old worn out watch?" She mocked disappointment.

"Hey sweetie, this here is an antique. A real oldie, but goodie."

"Maybe to you. I saw one exactly like it at the county fair last summer. Besides, it's only gold plated. There isn't an ounce of real gold in the whole thing. Hmm, too bad. I thought it might be a valuable piece. Guess I'll wait until the fair comes back to town." She turned to leave.

"Hey, no! Wait. Uh, I'll make ya a swell deal, and ya won't have to wait one day."

An exaggerated sigh escaped, and she sauntered back to the partition. "Well, I don't know. What kind of *deal* do you mean?"

"Since I'm Honest John and all, how 'bout two hundred and fifty bucks?" He spit the cigar into an ashtray.

"Did I hear you say twenty five dollars?"

"Aw, come on darlin'. I gave the guy two crisps Benjamins. I gotta make a little dough with overhead and all here at my establish, uh, I mean, business place."

Taste of Fire

A finger tapped the glass. "I happen to know the old coot. He scammed you, Johnny. You've been duped. He has no intentions of coming back for that piece of crap watch. Good day."

A pudgy hand smacked the counter, and the cash registered clanked open. "You drive a hard bargain, but I guess we've got a deal."

Back in the car, Terri jerked the gearshift into reverse. *What in the world could ever make you part with this Frank? It belonged to your Grandfather.*

TASTE OF FIRE
CHAPTER TWENTY

Several cars and trucks filled the lot outside of the Short Cut Bar and Grill by the time Terri arrived. Some belonged to fellow firemen and even a couple of police. *Great. Looks like a good crowd tonight.* She stared at the building. It seemed so much bigger as a little girl.

Charles Neal called Friday night Date Night. After work, he always took his daughter for a burger and fries. Swept up in large arms, he would carry Terri over one shoulder while she squealed and giggled. Once inside the Short Cut, he'd plop her down at the end of the counter and say to Frank, "I want to trade in this here sack of potatoes for a burger. How 'bout it?"

Frank would reply, "Sounds great. I need some potatoes to chop up for more French fries. Dump it in the storage room." *Blissful memories cherished forever.*

Terri retrieved the gold watch from her purse. Tiny scratches etched both sides of the slick metal from being taken in and out of Frank's pant pocket. The outside design captured intricate details of an eagle with wings spread wide, talons clamped around an arrow and a laurel wreath. It popped open. Faded black roman numerals graced the round white face and a broken chain dangled from the stem. Engraved in the lid were the words: *To William Franklin Gunnison with all my love, Lillie.*

"Frank, I guess you were named after your grandfather. No wonder you value this so much." The vintage heirloom slipped into a zippered compartment of the purse.

Laughter and music filled the lively club. A couple of the people threw up a hand and several nodded as Terri entered.

TASTE OF FIRE

The jukebox cranked out some country songs, and billiard balls thudded across the felted tabletop.

"Hey, welcome back to the Short Cut Bar and Grill." Frank's eyes twinkled.

"Thanks. How's my favorite shot-up, banged-up buddy?" she teased.

"Today my knee bothers me more than the shoulder, but I'm gonna make it. I had to get this place back to life. No money, not funny." He grinned. "You want something to drink? By the way, how are ya, and how is Doc?"

"A cola would be great." She scooted onto a stool. "Funny you should ask. I came here to tell you we went out on our date the other night."

He placed an iced mug on the counter and popped the top of the cold drink can. "Really? And …"

"And, I think the crowd is picking up. Maybe you'll be back to speed before long."

"Don't go messing with me, Little T. I'm dying to know if you and him hit it off or not." He pointed a finger.

"Well yes, we 'hit it off', as you put it, and enjoyed the night. We dined at La Petite St. Simone."

Frank whistled. "Yikes. Doc put down some bills at that fancy joint."

She slipped the paper off a straw. "It caused a ruckus at work, though."

"What? Do you have admirers in the Station House I don't know about? Who? Tell me who?"

"No, silly goose. There aren't any admires there, but the two dozen yellow roses Tucker sent the next day were a little hard to cover up. He even brought a huge bouquet to the house *before* the date."

TASTE OF FIRE

"Ah, so he did take my advice." An eyebrow rose. "Now, don't dilly-dally around. He's a keeper in my book," Frank added.

"Hey, what about me?"

"You? You're just an ornery, spoiled brat, but I love you. Thing is, we ain't neither one gettin' any younger. Face it, I won't always be around to take care of ya, so I gotta get cha married off." A hearty chuckle followed.

Terri stuck out her tongue.

"Now, now, mind those manners."

"Well, I wanted to talk to you about something else."

"Can't imagine anything more important than your love life, but go ahead—got both my ears on."

Terri took a sip and began, "The weirdest thing happened today at work. We responded to a house fire over on North Claude Street. Lightning struck a tree and caught the roof of a house on fire. An elderly black man lived there and remembered his cat was still inside. The blaze was intense when we arrived, but I rushed in to get the pet."

"That doesn't surprise me one bit."

"Listen, Frank. About the time I located the cat, a ceiling joist cracked and fell. It trapped me with the kitten in my arms."

"Oh sweet Jesus." A hand covered Frank's mouth.

"Obviously, they got me out. However, moments before, something bizarre occurred." She paused. "I saw it."

"Saw what?"

"Daddy's face, Frank. It was my daddy's face. He spoke, gave me a message. He even recounted that I'm special, and the fire is afraid of me—just like he explained over the years how I got my scar." Eyes

113

glassy, she stared into space as if reliving the event. "He held my hands. My feet were on top of his, and we danced."

"Holy moley, I can't believe it."

"I know—quite a shocker."

"No, no. The other night I had a dream. Chuck was bigger than life. We were out fishing on a lake somewhere. Remember when he'd say he wanted to go 'cast a few'?"

"Yes, his way of relaxing after a tough day at work," Terri replied.

"Right. Well, all of a sudden I saw these waves of fire. He spoke, calm, but stern. Told me not to let anything happen to *our* little girl." The words trailed off.

Amid the clatter of dishes, the sizzle of the grill, and loud music, they stared at each other.

"Something isn't right. Maybe it's an omen. We have to be careful. The fact someone tried to kill you was horrific. I lost my daddy. I can't lose you, too," her voice broke.

Frank leaned over the counter, and they hugged. "There, there, Little T. I ain't going nowhere. Besides, I need to see how this new fella I fixed ya up with fairs. If he's got common sense mixed in with all the doctor knowledge, he'd be smart to do some heavy courting."

"Courting? Talk about a word from the dark ages."

The older man tried to act perturbed, but started to chuckle. The ring of his cell phone interrupted their moment of amusement.

Terri watched the color drain from his face when Frank glanced at the caller ID.

TASTE OF FIRE

"Uh excuse me. I gotta take this call. Can you tend to business for a bit?" He walked into the storage room.

Anxiety settled over her. She slid off the barstool, eased close to the storage door entrance, and strained to hear.

"Look, I told you that's all I can send. I hocked my watch today. I'll wire the money and what I take in tonight, but you have to give me more time."

Frank mumbled something more, but the clamor in the bar drowned out the words.

"Everything okay?" She took another sip of the cola as Frank returned.

"Oh, yeah. Uh, one of my, uh vendors—said he'd be here tomorrow to make a delivery. Gosh, I really needed him to show up tonight. "His hands shook as he wiped off the counter.

What little of the conversation was audible might explain Frank's trip to the pawnshop, but she needed more. An idea formed, and she riffled through the purse. "Oh, for pity's sake."

"What's wrong?"

"I guess I left my phone at work."

"Well, I'm sure it'll be okay. Can't you swing by there on the way home?" Clean glasses clanked as he filled up a tray.

"Well, I suppose so, but I really wanted to call Tucker." A finger tapped the counter. "Could I borrow yours right quick?"

"Sure you can."

In a pretense of dialing, Terri hit caller ID. It read, *Orin Chambers*.

"You know what? I really want a little privacy. I'd better call him from the house. Thanks. See you later."

115

CHAPTER TWENTY ONE

The low hum of the ceiling fan paddled through the silence of the bedroom, and a light breeze circled around. Tucker stripped off his clothes and slid into bed. The crispness of the sheets felt cool against bare skin. Restless, he tried to relax, but found it impossible to get comfortable. A quick kick and the covers flew back.

A long breath escaped as he draped an arm over his eyes seeking the solace of sleep. All too soon, the hours to slumber would slip away like a kite caught by a brisk wind. But he couldn't forget the images of Terri Neal.

Even in the blank darkness, he could see her angelic face, eyes dark and energetic, feel the silkiness of her skin as though she were there, lying next to him. The damp curls on her forehead, the fragrance of her hair, and the taste of her kiss etched forever in his mind — and heart.

A successful career was always the paramount goal. Now, established and recognized in his field, he delighted in a bounty of satisfaction, and contentment … at least until one fateful night in the emergency room. Of course, there had been others, but no one serious, no one special for a long time. Now, one cute brunette firefighter was in the picture. Cilla Wisner would never know how her death brought new life into his own.

However, the dinner date at La Petite St. Simones changed every priority, every necessity, and every idea. The blind date, Frank so cunningly arranged, yielded much more than he could have imagined and

Taste of Fire

confirmed what he already knew … Dr. Tucker Abraham was in love.

He flipped on his stomach and buried his face into a big, square marshmallow pillow. The muscles in his body twitched, ached to be with her once more. *There are so many things I want to share. I need to hear her voice.* On one elbow, Tucker pushed up to grab the cell phone from the nightstand, but dropped back down on the bed. It was late. He'd call in the morning. Tomorrow was a special day, and hopefully he could include her in it.

◆◆◆◆

The metal cabinet rattled like a tin can as Terri forced it shut and twirled the combination lock. She sat down on the bench, hands over her face. Graveyard shift ended, and it'd been quiet, no call outs. Any other time, she'd be grateful a break, but sleep eluded and allowed anxiety to run rampant. Now, in the brightness of a new day, her head throbbed.

In the kitchen of the Station House, she grabbed a can of soda. The top popped, and the fizzy soft drink bubbled over the edge. She took a quick gulp. Normally, strong coffee started the morning, but she didn't want to stay for breakfast with the day shift crew. Perhaps caffeine from the soda would help the headache.

I have to find out what forced Frank to pawn the watch. Maybe I should talk to Tucker about it. The mere mention of his name brought a tingle. Life took on a different perspective since the good doctor came into view.

◆◆◆◆

At the nurse's station, Tucker jotted down notes for the patient in room 480. A glance at his watch documented the time. Suddenly, two soft hands folded around his eyes.

"Guess who?"

"Uh, let me see, is it Jennifer Lopez?" he said sternly.

"No."

"Marilyn Monroe?"

"Nope. Guess again."

"Hmm, it isn't Pamela Anderson because I would be able to feel two big boobs in my back," he teased.

"Tucker," the voice squealed.

He turned around and grabbed the girl up in his arms. Her feet dangled in the air. She was tall with straight brown hair down to the middle of her back and hips that tapered into long shapely legs.

"So, this is the big day, right?" He flashed a smile and released the hug.

"That is it. Now, *you* won't be the only medical person in our family, big brother." Navy blue eyes mirrored his.

"Goodness, it seems like only yesterday I was helping Mom change those stinky old diapers on you and Sheridan."

She slammed a knuckle into his forearm.

"Ouch, that hurt McKenzie Rene Abraham." Tucker held his arm and feigned injury.

"Well, don't you dare treat me like a little kid anymore," she huffed. "Are you going to be at the academy tonight to see me walk across the stage and receive my nursing degree? It starts at six o'clock."

◆◆◆◆

At the information desk in the foyer of Griffin County Hospital, Terri paused.

TASTE OF FIRE

"May I help you?" A woman dressed in a volunteer smock smiled.

"Yes ma'am. Can you check to see which floor Dr. Abraham is working today?"

"Sure, just a moment," she replied.

"They have him on the fourth floor this morning. Is it an emergency? He's on call, too," the woman offered.

"No ma'am, it isn't. Thank you."

"I'll be glad to page him for you, dear."

"No, that won't be necessary. Thank you again." Terri turned to walk away.

"Just go down this hall and make a right, and the elevators will be on your left," she continued.

"Yes, I know. Have a good day."

Terri thought about Margie and Gladys, the exuberant volunteers, and how helpful they were while Frank was hospitalized. *Oh Tucker, I can't wait to talk to you. I feel close enough to confide my concerns about Frank and the watch, as well as his dream and my vision in the fire.*

Impatient, yet excited, she punched the round number four in the elevator. It seemed to stop on every floor, and people moved on and off in slow motion. With a little luck, Tucker might be available for a chat. *This is a good excuse to cash in on the rain check for our coffee date.* She needed moral support, reassurance, and help to figure out the peculiar circumstances, but moreover, she wanted to be near him again.

The elevator chimed twice, and the doors finally opened on the fourth floor. As she rounded the corner, amid the traffic of hospital personnel, she could see Tucker with a dark haired woman at the other end of the hall. Even in a crowd, his presence was compelling.

Taste of Fire

Then astonishment erupted, she gasped and felt the blood drain from her face. Like a stone statue, she watched him pull the girl close, hands on her shoulders. He leaned down and kissed her forehead. Terri stood numb, frozen at the scene.

The attractive girl smiled and waved as she walked off.

"I can't wait to see you tonight at six, **Nurse McKenzie**," he called out.

She shrunk back around the corner, fell against the wall, jaw clenched to kill the sob in her throat. *I have to get away, run fast. If I could only disappear from sight, become invisible.*

A ladies restroom provided the nearest safe haven. The door shut, and trembling fingers turned the lock. Slowly, Terri slid down the beige painted wall to the floor. Mascara stained tears fell as she shook her head. *Stupid, stupid, stupid. How could you have been so blind? It didn't mean a thing to him. The emotions he said he felt, the terms of endearment that rolled so easy off his tongue were all idle words to get what he wanted. Why couldn't I see it was a one-night stand? Obviously, Nurse McKenzie is the next target of choice. And you, who never cries over a man, what's wrong with you?*

Nausea overpowered the emotions as she lunged toward the sink basin, gagging and heaving. A wet paper towel dabbed her cheeks and cherry red nose. More shaken than she wanted to admit, her heart refused to believe what her eyes witnessed. *I've guarded my heart for a long time. Now, just when I thought there was one decent man left in the world, I was wrong. The only person to fill those shoes was my daddy, and he's dead!*

Taste of Fire

She dug through her purse for a compact when something caught her eye, Wade's card. *Okay, fine. I can move on, too, Dr. Tucker Abraham.*

Taste of Fire
CHAPTER TWENTY TWO

The harmonic rumble from the exhaust brought a euphoria feeling as Terri gunned the accelerator of the Mustang. A peek around the tractor-trailer ahead revealed a large gap in the oncoming traffic. She forced the gas pedal downward, excitement surged. The car whipped in front of the eighteen-wheeler and back into the right-hand lane with ease.

It was good to have a little time off again, leave the concerns over Frank, and the disappointment from Tucker, behind. Without telling either, she packed a bag and left. A trip back to Skirts and Spurs might be the right therapy. Work left little time for friends, and she needed to talk to another female—Mom. *Even though our friendship is new, I have to get a few things off my chest. Maybe together, we can determine some logic to the mess in my life.*

"Well hello, Lou." Weston stood in the doorway of the club and tipped his hat.

Terri smiled and tossed the keys. It was quiet an ego boost he remembered her.

Although early, a large group already crowded the huge dance hall. She scanned the room. Over at the stage, Wade was busy setting up the sound system and didn't see her approach.

"Do you think a girl could get the band to play a request?"

Down on one knee, he looked over his shoulder. "Lou, great to see you again. Yes, the band is always yours." Standing, cowboy hat in one hand, the other behind his back, he gave a gallant bow like before. "It was a pleasant surprise to get the phone call. I wondered if you'd ever come back for an encore."

TASTE OF FIRE

"Did you, now? I'm sure you've had plenty of other singers since I was here last."

"Nope. I don't do favors for just anyone."

"Oh, so it was a favor? Not an honor?" She pretended to be annoyed.

"Girl, I can't ever win an argument."

"That's right, Mr. Wade, and don't you forget it." She laughed.

"Well, how about giving an old cowboy the pleasure of a dance?"

"I have to earn the right to perform with the band?"

"No ma'am, but I sure would like for us to scoot a boot or two. What do you say?" He turned to the musicians, gave some instructions, and took her arm. Are you ready?" A warm smile searched her eyes.

"How could a girl resist?" A hand in his, they moved across the floor to the slow strains of a waltz. He slid an arm around her waist. When he pulled her close, she felt relaxed in the cushioned embrace. There seemed to be a comfortable bond between the two.

The dance ended, and Wade brushed back the hair from her shoulders. "I really want you to sing again. Name the song, and I'll get Mama's Boys ready. How 'bout it, Lou?" he whispered.

The closeness brought a renewed strength. For an instant, she didn't want it to stop, but the truth was Wade didn't even know her real name.

Once again, Terri took the stage and performed to an explosive audience. The attention provided a sense of gratification, but in her heart, she knew it wasn't an appreciative crowd that prompted a trip back to Georgia.

She wiggled through the patrons toward the bar in the back. The line was long and every stool taken.

Taste of Fire

When she made it to the counter, Mom nodded. "Well Lou, what a pleasant surprise. It's so good to see you again. Loved the song you sang, too."

"Yeah, I think I'm getting addicted to this place for some reason."

"Must be the throng of cowboys at your feet." The woman winked. "I also saw you dancing with Wade. You know he's pretty much a rascal, don't cha?"

"Aren't they all?"

"Honey, sounds like you've already got 'em figured out." She laughed.

"Mom, when your shift is over can we go eat at that little restaurant like before? My treat. Besides, it'll be fun to chat some more."

"What a great offer, sweetie. I didn't have time to grab a bite before I came to work, so I'll be famished for sure by then. Think ya can afford to feed a starving old woman?"

"Hey, I have a healthy appetite, too." Terri took the first empty stool. "Wade wants me to sing another song. Guess I could put a tip glass on the edge of the stage to fund our feast. What do you think?"

"Good idea. Those silly men will be fighting over who can cram in the most greenbacks." She handed her an empty jar from behind the counter. "It might smell a bit like pickles, but I doubt anyone will notice."

They laughed, and Terri watched the sparkle in Mom's eyes as they talked. *I need this new friend in my life. Can I dare confide in you, though? I've lied about my name. Will you believe me if I tell the truth now?* "When it's time to leave, I'll wait at the back door again, okay?"

TASTE OF FIRE

"Sure thing. Now, get out there and have a good time." She went back to filling shot glasses and tossing longnecks.

Life wasn't easy growing up without a mother, and even though it felt a bit odd to call someone *Mom*, it actually made her feel good to say the word. *I wish it wasn't always a weekend adventure to bring us together.*

Terri danced with several cowboys, as well as Wade a few more times, but kept a watchful eye on the time. Midnight couldn't come soon enough.

She gave in to Wade's wishes and sang another song. The music and the people surrounded her, but Frank's circumstances, and the devastation from Tucker's deceitful actions, hindered the ability to enjoy the night.

The desire to spill everything to Mom grew, but the fact she lied about her own name gnawed at her conscience. *Am I truly any different from Tucker or Frank?*

Ridiculous thoughts whirled. She could make up a fake life for Lou—like the one she dreamed of as a little girl, but the truth was always best. It was only supposed to be one weekend of fun. How could she have known a cherished friendship would form?

A thin smile crossed her lips at the thought of Wade and those animated bows. How did he fit into all this? Was Mom being a bit protective warning her about him or just making a silly joke?

"Last call for alcohol and last dance of the night," resounded over the microphone.

Good, time for some honesty, and if this woman still acts as if she cares about me, I believe I've made a true friend.

Taste of Fire
CHAPTER TWENTY THREE

Wade and Weston reached the back exit the same time Terri and Mom started out the door. "Are you ladies headed to the all night café?" Wade grinned.

"Yeah, do ya'll plan to meet us?" Loretta spoke up. "You don't care if the guys go, too, do you, Lou?"

Terri lowered her eyes and didn't reply. *Company wasn't in the plan.*

"Honey, I asked if it was okay for the boys to meet us. If you don't want them, we can find somewhere else. However, at this late hour, the choices are limited."

"Oh no, that's fine. Uh, why don't you ride with me, so we can have some girl talk before they show up?"

"Not a problem, honey. For darn sure, nobody's gonna try to steal my old rattletrap even if I left it here all night."

"Yeah, right. Don't let her fool you, Lou. She wouldn't get rid of that jalopy if you *gave* her the six winning lottery numbers," Weston said.

"Is there some sentimental value there?" Terri empathized. She felt the same about her Mustang.

"Nay," Loretta replied.

"Go on and confess," Wade urged. "See, it was the first thing our dad bought her."

"You'd think it was gold or something. Mom could buy any new car on the lot, but refuses," Weston added.

"Your, you have a dad?" The heavy lashes that shadowed her cheeks flew up, eyes wide at the comment.

"Oh nonsense, silly boys. I don't want another payment is the reason I won't get rid of it," Loretta said. "Waymon Carter was a good man and father. It's been a while though since his death."

Wade's voice broke the uncomfortable silence, "Yeah, but Mom makes up for the void."

Weston leaned in to hug the older woman.

"Let's go, Lou. These guys know the way."

I've been so selfish and absorbed in my own situations, I didn't give much thought to the life and circumstances of anybody else.

An impromptu scheme developed. *What about a visit in Anniston? Truth is, she's a good woman who needs a good man, and I happen to know a great one ... Frank.* One thing for sure, the truth needed revealing to straighten out things—and before Wade and Weston joined them.

The two women climbed into the sports car. Terri turned the key in the ignition, and Loretta shook her head.

"Is there something wrong?"

"I can't tell you how this takes me back to a time in my youth," the woman said softly.

"Oh, this car? Yeah, I love it like you do yours."

"Most kids your age like the jacked-up trucks or SUV's—something to show status. Only a few drive what we used to call muscle cars." Loretta smiled. "Are you an old soul?"

"Hmm, never heard the term, but I like it." They pulled away from the club. "Tell me again how to get there."

"Take the main highway back east. It's not very far, down on the right. The crowded parking lot will be the giveaway." Loretta's seat belt clicked.

Terri decided to start the much-needed conversation before they arrived. "Loretta, I mean, Mom, I have to be honest with you. The reason I came back to Skirts and Spurs was totally to see you again." She pulled into traffic.

"Me? Don't you mean Wade? You know he hasn't stopped talking about you since ya'll met. He was pretty excited to get that call."

"He told you I called?"

"Sure, my boys and I are very close. Well, actually stepsons, however, I love them as if they were my own. I feel certain he thought you wouldn't mind. Are you upset?"

"Gracious no. I love the fact they're respectful and protective." She changed lanes, silent for a moment. After a sideways glance, she spoke, "I have some news to share with you. It might be quite a surprise."

"Dear Jesus, Lou. Please don't tell me you're pregnant."

"What?" her voice rose.

"I'm teasing you, baby. You need to lighten up. I know Wade is sweet on you, but at least I didn't think you two had gotten together. Am I wrong?" There was now a tone of anxiety in the older woman's voice.

"Oh, no ma'am, but my name, well it isn't Lou … I made it up. See, I needed to get away from my stressful job. I wanted to be a total stranger, anonymous, if you will." Stopped at a red light, Terri touched the older woman's hand.

"Guess I needed a friend, and from the minute we met, there seemed to be a connection. Hope it's okay to admit all this. There's a lot going on in my life right now. Truth is, I needed a confidant."

"Sweetie, I didn't believe it was your name from the very beginning, but I get that a lot. Something told me you were different. Wasn't any of my business to ask questions though. However, I'm honored you feel close. Just so you know, I felt the same bond. After we didn't see you again, I dismissed it from my silly head."

The light changed, and Terri listened as they continued down the highway.

"There was a time in my life when I needed the same type of closeness, but I ran away. It seemed like the right move for everyone involved. To be honest, I have a lot of regrets." They travelled in silence for a while. "See, I use to drink, but there was a good reason. I know that's what everyone claims, but I was trying to mend a broken heart. Instead, I wound up breaking the hearts of the people who really loved me," her voice cracked.

"Anyway, I straighten up my life, and God blessed me with a wonderful man, Waymon Carter, the epitome of a southern gentleman who treated me like a real lady. The twins were fairly young, and their mother had lost a long battle with cancer. Those boys were just an added bonus for me. Don't misunderstand—I cared for the man deeply. Problem was I only had one true love, the kind every girl dreams of finding. I did love Waymon, just wasn't *in* love with him." She grabbed a tissue from her purse. "Mercy, listen to me rattling away. You wanted to talk, and I've hogged up the whole conversation."

"No, I'm glad you shared such private thoughts."

"After he died, the boys and I bought Skirts and Spurs, sunk every dime, but it's been a prosperous venture. 'Course, I couldn't do it alone. They work very hard, the little scoundrels, and this way I can keep an eye on 'em." She chuckled. "Honestly though, they've become very dependable businessmen, and we enjoy being together. What about you?"

Taste of Fire

Tears ran down Terri's cheeks.

"Baby girl, what's wrong?"

"Oh Mom, I ran away from someone I love, too, at least I thought I loved him."

"There, there. Here, have a tissue. Do you want to talk about it?"

Terri dabbed her eyes. "He's a doctor, and this might sound silly, but it's like fairies taking flight every time he's near. However, yesterday I went to the hospital and, well …" she sniffed.

"Let me guess—was he talking to another woman?"

CHAPTER TWENTY FOUR

Trucks, cars, and big rigs filled the parking lot at the Red Cup Café. After a couple circles through the crowded area, Terri found an open space and squeezed the small car between a mud covered pick-up and an oversized SUV.

Questions weighed heavy. The twins would show up soon, and this conversation was personal, private. Nervous, she said a little prayer. "Mom, before we go inside, I want to mention something without the guys in earshot."

"Okay, dear, go ahead."

"Our friendship is new, but we confessed there's a mutual union, right?" A deep breath helped suppress the apprehension.

"Yes. Might sound silly, but your spunkiness sorta reminds me of myself many years ago. I love those stinking boys, but it's nice to have female around."

"Well, are you up for a dare?" A sly grin formed.

"Oh heavens, I don't know so much about a dare."

"Perhaps the word is a bit intense. Let me explain. There's someone I want you to meet. Don't say no yet; let me tell you about him."

"Meet? Who? Spit it out 'cause I never was good at reading between the lines." Her eyes widened.

"There's a gentleman, a good man, who is like an uncle to me. I don't have any family left, so our friendship is special. Since my daddy died, he's been somewhat of a surrogate father, always looking out for me, there when I need a friend, that sort of thing. He even introduced me to the doctor I mentioned. He's a business owner, hard worker, and a great person." She watched the woman's dark eyes sparkle. "He doesn't know anything about you. I never told him, or anyone else, about my trip to Atlanta." The seat belt unbuckled. "I'd like to introduce him to you. Will you please take a chance?"

"Can I fill in the blanks?"

"Sure." Leary, Terri crossed her fingers.

"First off, if it means this much for me to meet your friend ... I'm game."

"Oh great," she squealed.

"Hey, I ain't getting any younger. However, I do have a suggestion."

"Sure, this will all be on your terms."

"On the subject of the doctor, why don't you go to the guy, give him a chance to explain? You're a smart cookie. If he tries to play you for a fool, you'll figure it out. Don't be so quick to judge. It might prove a pleasant surprise to find those suspensions were wrong. Sometimes, you have to give a person the benefit of the doubt. All too often, we learn things the hard way. Lord knows, it nearly cost me the life of my ... uh, niece."

"Your niece?"

"Well yes, I have a sister, and I, uh, I mean she was so messed up. The next thing I know, she gave her ex-husband the rights to that precious child. It was such a stupid, stupid decision, but I understand now. My sister thought the father was the only one who could take care of the little girl." She paused. "Looking back, perhaps it was true. Later, we learned he filed a permanent injunction. No one will ever understand how I grieved over such injustice."

"I'm sorry. I never meant to pry into your past." Terri patted her hand. "Sounds like you loved her as if she were your own."

Taste of Fire

"Lou, life is what you make it. I was a wild thing growing up. My family disowned me because I took off with a friend, thought I'd go to Hollywood, and become an actress. After that disastrous episode, going back home was not an option. Alcohol provided an escape, but led to lots of mistakes. I made a bargain with God. Thank goodness for His redeeming grace. He answered my prayers and brought Waymon in my life." A smile appeared. "You'll find your special person one day, too."

Terri shook her head. "I thought I already had. How does a girl know when she's found Mr. Right?"

"It's really simple. When he's near, your whole body will tingle. Heck, even your toes will have butterflies." She leaned back against the headrest. "Gracious, as much as Waymon held my heart, even now the mere thought of my first love makes me giddy."

A rap on the driver side window interrupted. Two handsome cowboys peered back.

"Those guys are probably starving. Better go in and get 'em some breakfast."

"Sure." Terri nodded.

As she started to get out of the car, Mom touched her shoulder. "Don't forget what I said about benefit of the doubt, and by the way, I'll keep calling you *Lou* until you decide to tell me your real name, okay?"

◆◆◆◆

Several people spoke as they entered the restaurant. Loretta smiled and threw up a hand. She was tired, but the conversation with Lou kindled memories engrained on her heart, never to return, or so she thought.

TASTE OF FIRE

Ordinarily, the suggestion of meeting a complete stranger would have rallied a quick 'no way'. However, the fact this girl walked into her life on a whim stirred some unanswered questions. She needed to follow a gut feeling. Common sense demanded she press Lou for a real name, but for some reason, she really didn't care.

Skirt and Spurs developed into a very lucrative adventure with Wade and Weston as business partners. They seemed to inherit their father's business savvy. Good guys, so protective and always looking after her. *Wonder how they'll react to my teenybopper answer to meet Lou's uncle?*

She bit a lip as the idea loomed. Had she acted too quickly, or was there a good reason to follow a hunch? *Lord have mercy, Loretta. What kind of mess have you gotten yourself into, girl? He could be some sort of pervert or try to screw you out of your business or, or, or ..."*

"Mom, gonna stare at the menu until dawn, or do you want one of us to order for you?" Weston teased.

Lost in thought, Loretta didn't notice the waitress impatiently tapping her pencil on the order pad. "Sorry, guess I'm more tired than I realized. Give me a couple of scrambled eggs, bacon, toast, and lots of black coffee."

The girl retrieved the menu. "Coulda just said you wanted the Breakfast Deal Number Two."

When the foursome took the semi-circular booth in the back, Wade slid in beside Terri.

Loretta quickly shot her a wink.

"So Lou, how is that doctor friend of yours?" She opened up the wrapped silverware.

"Uh, he works long hours, but we still see quite a bit of one another."

TASTE OF FIRE

"What? You have a boyfriend?" the comment came from the other twin.

"Well yes, yes I do."

"Damn it," Weston added.

"Wes, watch your language," Loretta interrupted.

"I apologize, but I was hoping you would fall for my stupid brother. He probably won't admit it, but he needs some class in his life." A jab in the rib from Wade made Weston wince. "Ouch."

"Shut up you idiot. I don't need you dissecting my social life." Wade glared.

"Lou and I are not going to listen to any silly squabble between two grown men. Ya'll hear me?" Loretta's voice rose.

Terri touched Wade's shoulder. "This is my fault. Please, let me explain. I came back to Skirts and Spurs to see Mom. I mean, I wanted to see all three of you again. You were kind enough to give me your business card, so I called."

"What did you say to blow it, oh smart brother of mine?" Weston quipped.

Before a reply came, Loretta snapped her fingers. "What did I just say?"

"Wait; let me try to clear up the confusion." A hand raised in protest. "Guys, I don't have a mother, well, I do, but I don't know if she is dead or alive. The friendship I developed with yours is very important to me. You, Wade, were just the icing on the cake, and I am so flattered. However, I'm seeing someone." She glanced at Loretta. "Like I said, he's a doctor, and things are pretty serious. Still, a girl can't have too many friends. We *are* still friends, right?"

"Hey, what about me?" Weston pushed his cowboy hat back.

TASTE OF FIRE

"Of course, you, too. I could never leave out anyone who gives me such grand wolf whistles."

"I can't say I'm not disappointed, Lou, but I understand. We're still good." Wade put an arm around her shoulder and gave a squeeze. "Shoulda known you'd snag somebody like a doctor. He better be good to you, or he'll have to answer to the Carter wrath."

Loretta watched the twinkle in Wade's eyes. *My boys are going to make some lucky girls great husbands one day.*

❖❖❖❖

The food orders arrived, and conversations bounced from chatter to laughter. When they finished, Terri knew it was time to bring up the invitation offered earlier. The waitress brought refills, and the subtle aroma of coffee helped calm the jitters. How would these caring sons react?

"Guys, I have to confess something."

"Heck, I don't think my old bro here can stand anything more devastating than the doctor beau revelation," Weston replied.

Wade frogged his brother's arm. "Keep yer trap shut, you loon."

"Boys?" Loretta's eyebrow rose.

It's okay, Mom, in fact, I sorta like their banter. Not having any siblings growing up, this is pretty good entertainment." Terri giggled. "On a serious note though, I want you to know, I asked Mom to meet a friend of mine. He's an older, single gentleman and very dear friend, like family. Would either of you have any objections?"

The boys looked at one another and then to Loretta.

TASTE OF FIRE

"Well, I'd like to know a little more about him, but I guess in all honesty that'd be up to her," Weston replied.

"She knows my opinion," Wade added. "I have been telling her for a while she should get out there and date, but she spends every spare second working."

"Good point, Wade, and I agree." Terri gulped down the last swallow of coffee. "Well, by now you know I don't live here. Actually, I have a home outside of Anniston, and I'd like for Mom to come back with me for a couple of days to meet him. He owns his own business, a little restaurant of sorts, and can make a mean hamburger." Terri licked her lips.

"So, does this friend know about *her*?" Wade crossed his arms.

"Oh no, I haven't said a word, but I know he wouldn't object. He's been alone along time, too. In fact, he never married. He told me once, after he missed the chance to marry the girl he really loved, he stopped looking. If they don't hit it off, so be it, but who knows? At least you would have made a new friend, and like I said …"

"You can never have too many friends," all four said in unison.

Their laughter filled the café, and several patrons stared.

"What's the verdict?"

"A couple days or so?" Weston replied.

"Yes, unless she wants to stay longer." Terri smiled at Loretta. "My house is open to any of you."

"I'm good, but how about you, Mom?" Wade winked. "Think you're up for a blind date?"

"I might still have a little charisma left in these old bones." She placed a hand on her hip. "One thing I do

137

know, I ain't getting any younger, and it ain't getting any earlier. Weston, why don't you take me back to get my car? Terri you follow Wade to the house. We're gonna get a little rest before ya drag this old woman out on a road trip. My blind date, my rules."

"Great, I'm tired, too. Wade just about danced the boots off me tonight." Terri kissed his cheek.

"Dang girl. You *sure* you got a boyfriend? I really do want you to get rid of, I mean, *date* my brother," Weston teased.

"Son, hush up and listen. While I'm gone, you boys better not be having any wild women over partying until the crack of dawn, understand?"

"The only two wild women I know will be headed to Anniston." Wade grinned.

CHAPTER TWENTY FIVE

A sprinkle of light from a crescent moon played hide and seek between plump clouds as Terri flipped the blinker on and turned off the county road behind Wade's truck. The tires rippled across a double cattle guard. At the entrance of an arched-pipe gateway, a large metal 'C' sat on top. Barbwire fences lined each side of the unlevel dirt drive, while a trail of dust from the pickup led the way.

Soon, a stucco ranch house cradled by pine trees came into sight. The vehicle stopped in front where security lights tinted the ground amber, and Terri parked alongside.

"Welcome to our humble abode." The truck door banged shut.

She took in a breath of night air. "It's lovely and peaceful here."

They stepped upon a wraparound porch to the welcome of several wooden rockers.

"Would you like to sit and wait for the rest of our motley crew? Shouldn't be long," Wade offered.

Cattle bawled, and owls hooted in the night. Across the fenced grassland, round hay bales looked like giant Tootsie rolls in the blackness.

A Catahoula hound appeared at the steps, lumbered onto the porch, and laid its head on Wade's knee. "Hey Oakley, I'd like you to meet Lou."

The dog ambled over to Terri and sniffed.

"Oakley? As in Annie?" She patted the brindle-colored fur.

"Yup, Mom's idea."

"Her eyes are so unusual, sorta blue-white."

"Yeah, they call those glass eyes, pretty common for the breed. Gotta say, ol' Oakley is the best watch dog we've ever owned."

"How's that? She didn't even bark when we arrived."

Oakley circled twice in front of Terri's chair and curled up in a ball.

"Oh, she picked up your scent the moment you got out of the car. Strangers don't always get the sort of greeting you received. The very fact she sat next to you means you passed *her* test." He grinned. "Otherwise, there would've been more than just barking."

The crunch of gravel made Oakley's ears twitch.

"See that little wiggle? Must mean Mom and Wade turned off the highway."

Moments later, Loretta's car puttered up the drive and rumbled to a halt. Weston climbed out, a brown bag in each hand.

"Come on in, Lou. I'll show you the guestroom." Loretta gestured. "Sorry it took us a bit longer. Needed to stop and get a few sundries at the 24-hour convenience store. *Somebody* drank up all the coffee … can't start my day without a hot cup of java."

"She'd be a little grumpy," Wade replied.

"Heck, more like an old grizzly bear, you mean," Weston added.

"Oh shush, before I ask our guest to fetch me a switch and tan both your hides." Loretta swatted toward the guys. "Did I tell you I killed a young sapling oak trying to raise these heathens?"

A small giggle escaped Terri's lips as Wade held the screen door open. "Better watch out. She's got a mean backhand."

TASTE OF FIRE

Inside, the rustic décor gave an air of coziness. A camel-colored, leather couch and wingback chairs surrounded a rough-wood coffee table. On each side of the large rock fireplace was a mounted deer head, hunter's trophies. A variety of photos sat staggered on the mantle—an embellished silver frame of a couple at a party, in the center.

Terri stopped to look.

"That was me and Waymon on our wedding day," Loretta said softly.

"What a lovely couple. I see the boys favor their dad." She ran a finger over the glass.

"Handsome men, even as little guys, I have to admit."

"Yes ma'am."

"Are we gonna have to listen to sentimental women talk?" Weston put an arm around Loretta, and she pinched his side.

"Ouch!"

"Mr. Smarty Pants go to bed."

"I'm going, I'm going, just don't pinch my fat again." He backed out of the room.

"See you ladies in the morning, and Lou, if you need anything, my room is next to yours." Wade tipped his hat and disappeared down the hall.

"I get up early regardless of the time I go to bed, but you can sleep in. Now, I'll expect you to eat a good hearty breakfast before we start out on this hair-brain adventure." She cupped a hand around her mouth and whispered, "But heck, I think it's gonna be fun."

After preparing the coffee pot, Loretta took Terri to the extra bedroom. "Okay honey, you'll find a cotton gown or two in the dresser, and there are sundries in the little bathroom. Make yourself at home. I have to say, it feels good to have another girl in the house."

The women hugged.

"Goodnight, or rather, good morning, and thanks for everything. I hope I can sleep because I'm really excited." Terri squeezed Loretta's hand and slipped into the guestroom.

Two dark green, needlepoint pillows rested next to the headboard of the oak and wrought iron bed. A white crocheted bed skirt adorned the bottom. Eyelet curtains matched sage-colored walls.

On top of the dresser sat a tattered, brown teddy bear. An anxious finger touched the raggedy toy. One side was rough, matted. *For some reason, this feels familiar.*

Inside the dresser drawer was a yellow print gown. The light material slipped over Terri's head, and she cuddled it to her body. *I wish this had been my room as a little girl; I love it.* Tired hands pulled back the star-pattern quilt, and she slid under the covers. Across the room, the worn stuff toy seemed to beckon. *This is probably silly, but ... no one will know.* She scampered over and retrieved it. Nestled in her arms, the bear brought warmth and sleep came easy.

The sharp crow of a rooster, and a rap at the door interrupted the serenity of a sleep. *What? I just closed my eyes.*

Loretta entered, coffee cup extended. "Oh good, you're awake. Did you rest okay?"

Terri shoved the old bear under her pillow. "Short and sweet." Propped against the headboard, she took a sip of the hot liquid. "I'm anxious for us to make this little jaunt."

TASTE OF FIRE

"Checked the news channel a bit ago. The weatherman said there's a good chance for heavy rain. Soon as you get ready and eat breakfast, we better get on the road. I'm already packed, but girl, I'm nervous." Loretta sighed.

Terri slid out of bed and gave her a hug.

"Mom, it'll be fine. I promise."

On the front porch, Oakley stood between the twins, tail wagging.

"I put your suitcase in the car. Drive safe, you two wild women." Wade waved.

"Don't hurry back," Weston quipped.

A few hours later, Terri glanced in the rearview mirror at the older vehicle. She kept a watchful eye not to lose sight of Loretta in traffic. She wanted them to ride together and offered to bring Mom back at the end of the visit, but Loretta insisted on taking her own car. *Can't blame her for being a bit apprehensive. If things don't feel comfortable, she can leave on her own timetable.*

By early afternoon, they neared the outskirts of Anniston. Ominous gray clouds hung low, and raindrops peppered the windshield.

Terri grabbed the cell phone and punched the number three on speed dial.

After several rings, Frank answered, "Short Cut Bar and Grill."

"Hey old man, what're you doing?"

"Little T? Where the heck are you? Tucker came in here yesterday, said he wanted to talk to you, see you again."

A cool chill ran over her skin at the mention of his name. *Well, he can wonder all he wants. I guess he had his fun with Nurse McKenzie, and now is back to me.*

"What'd you tell him?"

Taste of Fire

"I said maybe you went out of town. He mentioned some special plans, but couldn't get hold of you. The guy looked pretty disappointed," Frank continued.

"He didn't tell me about any special plans, besides I'm not so sure I have time for Tucker anymore."

"What? I thought you two really hit it off. I mean, I ain't seen you that happy in a while. Did you have a fight?"

"Frank Gunnison, don't be so nosey."

"Now listen, I care about the both of you. What happened? If he acted out of place, me and him will have a come to Jesus meeting, for sure."

Traffic slowed, and she adjusted the phone. "Oh Frank, I do like him, in fact I like him a lot, but I went to the hospital and there was someone else — a nurse. They acted very familiar, heads close, laughing. Maybe it's not meant to be, you know?"

"Look, you're all he talks about. He even called me at home, said he was checking in on me, but I knew better. Maybe you two need to get this out in the open. Could you have misunderstood?"

"I ... I don't know. It doesn't matter, and besides, I have something more important to talk about than Dr. Abraham."

"What do you mean?"

Excitement bubbled as she strategized how to explain the visitor coming to meet him. "Well, I left town to visit someone, a lady. Now, before you start to holler at me, listen to what I have to say, please."

"This sounds like the time I caught ya upon the bar stool, one hand in the tip jar. You said you needed a box of band-aids for a skinned knee from roller skating."

Taste of Fire

"Oh gracious, I forgot about that. I needed money because I wanted you to meet the cashier at the supermarket." She giggled.

"Yup, ya thought she needed a better job—at the Short Cut." Laughter erupted.

"I promise, Frank, no one is job hunting, but you do need to meet this woman. How about tonight … supper at Angelo's, the new Italian bistro downtown?"

"Little T, I think I'll turn you over my knee when you get here. Ain't no woman gonna be interested in an old man like me, especially one with a bum knee, not to mention a banged up shoulder. Have you lost all good sense, girl?"

"Trust me on this one. A good woman in life is hard to find, and she deserves a good man. Please? Nothing fancy or formal."

"Well …"

"Good. It's starting to rain, but we'll be at the Short Cut for one of your famous hamburgers in about thirty minutes, so act like a gentleman."

"I'd be a gentleman anyway, but now I feel like a silly teenager. I'm nervous, my hands are all sweaty, my stomach wants to flip-flop, and it's your fault."

Through the protest, she caught a touch of eagerness in his voice.

"Frank, you're so funny." Terri laughed as she approached the green light and a grid work of traffic. In an instant, a scream blazed through the phone. "Oh my God, Frank!"

TASTE OF FIRE
CHAPTER TWENTY SIX

A glimpse in the side mirror sent an icy surge of fear through Terri.

The diesel engine roared, and black smoke jutted from chrome pipe stacks, as the driver of a dump truck gunned the vehicle through the rain slick crossway.

No, no, please don't run the red light.

Loretta proceeded through the intersection on a green arrow, oblivious to any imminent danger.

No tires squealed, no horns blared ... only the crunch of metal and disintegrating glass. The impact spun the old car like a toy top and slammed it into the passenger side of a pickup. Both careened into a streetscape of light poles and concrete sidewalks. Shards of glass and raindrops pelted the asphalt in a luminescent array.

For a moment, it played before Terri as if in slow motion.

A deafening silence gave way to a warlike atmosphere. People screamed, others scattered, some fell to the ground, and a few shouted obscenities.

Terri fixated on the distorted scene. *Déjà vu – the death angel.* She gulped hard. *What have I done?*

Though lightheaded and nauseous, she elbowed through the crowd. "Let me through, let me through. I know this woman. Let me help."

A teenage boy in ripped jeans and black t-shirt made it to the massive destruction before her. He struggled to pry open the crumpled car door. One man produced a rusty crow bar, and with the help of another bystander, forced it open enough for Terri to wedge her body slightly inside the annihilated vehicle.

TASTE OF FIRE

Slumped over the steering wheel, Loretta lay unconscious. Two fingers probed for a pulse before Terri eased the limp body back in the seat. Blood covered the woman's face and gushed from her nose.

"Oh dear God!"

"Here, use this." The young boy jerked a yellow bandana from his pocket.

The sticky fluid made murky orange spots on the cloth as she caressed the older woman's face. "Mom, don't worry everything is going to be okay. I'll get Tucker, Dr. Abraham—he won't let anything bad happen," her voice cracked. "I'm sorry, so sorry. Hang in there, please."

Others assisted, and the twisted metal door groaned open. The all too familiar wail of sirens erupted while Terri fell to her knees and vomited.

◆◆◆◆

The automatic doors at Griffin County Hospital opened, and paramedics shouted out vital information. Medical personnel flooded around. In precision movements, they maneuvered the gurney inside.

Terri clenched Loretta's hand in a sprint alongside the stretcher.

They rounded the corner, and a voice called out, "Terri?"

Familiar blue eyes greeted her ... again. Dread and anger meshed. "Tucker, please, please, help us. I cannot lose her. Don't you dare let Mom die like you did Cilla," she demanded.

Outside the hospital, trees danced in circles whipped by the blustery wind, while sheets of rain malleated the ground. The waiting room grew more crowded as ambulance after ambulance brought in victims of Mother Nature's tantrum. People wandered in and out, children cried, and medical staff scurried.

Terri faced the window and watched enormous raindrops blast the square panes, collide with one another, and race downward.

"Little T?" Frank stood in the hall.

"Oh dear Lord, what have I done? It's all my fault." Arms flung around his neck.

For a moment, neither spoke.

"Now, now, it's gonna be okay."

"How can you be sure? What if she dies? No, she can't die."

"Your friend is in good hands. Tucker will do everything possible. He saved my life, right?"

She pushed back. "How did you know this is his shift?"

"He called, said he met the ambulance, and you needed me. Of course, your scream in the phone left me a bit deaf." Frank tried to grin. "I am a bit puzzled, though. Doc thought this lady was your mother, of all things. Come on, let's sit down. Tell me exactly what happened. Who is this person?"

Terri eased onto a couch near the corridor. "Remember when you told me I needed to have some real fun for a change? Well, I took your suggestion and went to the outskirts of Atlanta, to a place called Skirts and Spurs and ..." the words faded. "I have to call Wade and Weston! What an idiot I am. They need to be here for Mom, too." She scrambled through her purse.

"Who? Wade and who? What do you mean *Mom*?" Frank rubbed his forehead. "Did you fall on your head? What's all this nonsense about your mother?"

The questions went unanswered.

Wade's business card in hand, Terri dialed the number. Through choked words, details of the accident spilled.

Frank's eyes widened at the animated conversation.

"Yes, yes, Griffin County Hospital. It will take a few hours to get here. I know, I lied about my name. It's Terri, Terri Neal. We'll discuss it after you get here. Put on the emergency flashers and hurry, but please don't drive reckless. I need both of you safe." She slumped next to Frank on the couch.

"Okay young lady—my turn. I want to know everything about this woman, and who in the heck did you call?" his voice calm, but stern.

A ragged breath escaped as she settled against the vinyl cushion. "Wade and Weston Carter are the stepsons of Loretta Carter. I met them when I went to the club I mentioned, Skirts and Spurs. Everyone there calls Loretta *Mom*. The trip was fun, but other things evolved ... an unexpected union with her. The newfound relationship sorta filled a void in my life. After the incident of Tucker and the nurse, I needed another female to talk to, so I made a trip back."

"Okay, let me sort things out regarding Ms. Carter."

"Loretta," she whispered.

"Such a pretty name. Anyway, it's obvious she's special if you confided disappointment over Tucker. Got that part, but why bring her to Anniston?"

"For you ..." Terri rolled her eyes. "And I guess for me, too."

"Why for me?"

"If things worked out right, I thought I could have the two people who mean the most in my life, together." A hand massaged the back of her neck, eyes lowered. "This is hard to talk about, Frank. Plus, there's another aspect I need to confess." She turned to face him. "I think I'm in love with Tucker."

"What great news, young lady. Why haven't you told me this before?"

"Because of the scene at the hospital." She sighed.

"What? The nurse you mentioned? This man doesn't have time for another woman. Believe me; he only has eyes for you. Geez, the guy about drove me crazy asking where you were, had I heard from you, did I know why you left without a word. If it hadn't been my big idea for ya'll to get together, I'd be pretty annoyed by it all." A grin showed. "So, tell me about the nurse. I have a fan club in the hospital if you remember. Won't be hard for me to get a little insider information." He slapped his hands together.

"Tucker brought yellow roses to the house the night of our date, and the next day another huge bouquet arrived at the Station House. I wanted to thank him in person and came to the hospital. But as I rounded the corner, I saw him embrace some girl. They didn't see me, although I heard him call her name."

"What'd he say?"

"I'll see you later, Nurse McKenzie. She must work here. I bet he dates all the nurses. Whatever made me think I was so special? But I refuse to be a trophy for any man. Let's face it; our blind date was a one-time deal, a checkmark in his little black book which is probably stuck in the pocket of his lab coat."

Frank handed her a tissue, and she blew her nose.

"Yet, I can't deny every time he's close, I tingle all over. Mom did say it's a sure sign of love. I'm sure the handsome doctor makes all the women tingle."

"Oh sweetheart, you're wrong. He told me …"

Footsteps interrupted the conversation.

TASTE OF FIRE

"Frank, glad you're here." Tucker turned to Terri. "I need to talk to you about your mother, and here are her personal items." He held out a clear plastic bag.

As she took it, he placed a hand on hers. It was warm like the first night in the emergency room. *I need strength – his strength.*

"This horrible mess is because of me, entirely my fault," she whimpered.

An arm slipped around her shoulder, and he pulled Terri to his side. "Nothing is your fault, but what *is* important is your mother's health. There are no broken bones. That's the good news. Bumps and bruises will heal, and there are bandages on her face because of all the contusions. The bad news is there are internal injuries. Right now, she's in a coma."

"Oh no." Terri's knees buckled.

Tucker caught the limp body and eased her over to a couch. "Let me finish. It's an induced state to give us better control of vitals like in Frank's situation. The last thing we need is for her to go into shock. Now Frank, tell me what's her full name."

"Holy smokes, Doc, I never met the lady."

Terri kept a tight grip on Tucker's arm. "Loretta, Loretta Carter. I told Frank she has two stepsons, and I notified them. They're on the way, but live outside of Atlanta.

"If you're the closest relative, we need to get busy. I need a complete blood count and type done. Let's head to the lab."

"Wait, there ... there isn't any relation. We only met a short time ago."

"What? You told me not to let your Mom die."

"Look, it's kinda like a nickname. I brought her to Anniston to meet Frank, sort of a blind date, in the

151

hopes they might find what I thought you and I had," she spat.

Hands on both shoulders, he turned her toward him. "What do mean *had*?"

"I saw you, Tucker. I saw you with that nurse. Go ahead and admit it. I was a one-night stand." She jerked away.

"Terri, right now we need to find a kidney donor for your mother, or your friend, or whoever she is ... not waste time in an argument over something I don't even understand." Irritation rang in his voice.

"A kidney transplant?" Frank and Terri replied in unison.

"Blunt force trauma sustained from the crash catapulted her into renal failure. At present, both kidneys are nonfunctional. I don't have time to discuss our personal situation. I am in *love* with you, Terri Neal. I realized it after you came in with Cilla Wisner. I just haven't said it until this very second." He held a hand up in protest. "I'll repeat those three very special words for the rest of my life if you feel the same. Right this minute, a patient's life is in my charge. I have to act, or we might lose this woman."

Tucker's words stunned Terri, took her breath.

He turned to walk away.

"Wait." She ran to his side. "Test me."

"Dr. Abraham, Dr. Abraham," a heavy-set black nurse interrupted. "I have the National Kidney Foundation on the phone like you requested."

"Terri, if there's a donor in the area, you don't need to be tested. Besides, what if you are a match? Why would you go through such invasive surgery for a stranger?"

"She's not a stranger, she's a friend. I might not be a match, but you won't know unless you check. Right?" She placed a hand on his chest, and a tingle surged. *Loretta was right.*

CHAPTER TWENTY SEVEN

Papers and folders lay scattered across the mahogany desk while Tucker poured over the data. Two lengthy conference calls validated and reserved the necessary kidney for Loretta Carter. Also, a world-renowned specialist, Dr. Cleveland Lazaro was in flight to Griffin County Hospital, and the emergency operation scheduled in a couple hours. Anxiety and helplessness spurned an adrenaline flow. *I can't let the love of my life go through major surgery unnecessarily.*

An hour earlier, Terri stood toe to toe, adamant to donate a kidney. "Tucker, I have to do whatever I can to save this woman. Please, explain the choice for a good donor."

Those chocolate eyes penetrated his soul, but the words stung his heart as he watched her plead.

"In the decision for consideration as a donor, two initial blood tests are done to determine your blood type and the degree of HLA matching. Once the results of your blood typing and HLA matches are verified, the transplant staff will discuss the donation process and options to make an informed choice. All those conversations are strictly confidential," he began.

"Okay, I understand."

"Also honey, individual circumstances must be carefully evaluated."

"What do you mean?" Her brow furrowed.

"For example, can you take time off from work for surgery, and what about recovery at home? Things of this nature, and at that point, the rest of the evaluation will begin."

"What does the evaluation include?"

Tucker slid both hands in the lab coat pockets. "Well, the HLA tissue typing test, performed as part of the first step, shows how well you match the recipient. The blood cells are mixed with the serum of the recipient in a cross match test to see if the serum kills off your cells. If cells are destroyed, it means the immune system of the recipient would reject your kidney."

"What about these cross match tests? Tell me more," her voice rose.

"In most cases, they're repeated one or two weeks before the surgery because cross matches can change. It's a little tricky because even if it isn't favorable for a transplant now, there's always a chance it might be in the future. However, we do *not* have that sort of time for Loretta."

Terri walked to the window and stared at the rain, silent.

"Sweetheart, there's a lot to this you don't understand." He followed. "Once the tissue typing and cross matches are determined, you'd have to see a transplant nephrologist at the nearby medical clinic. Also, your own primary care physician needs to compile a complete medical history, not to mention perform a physical to see if you have any health present or hereditary conditions that might present a problem."

"Is that all?" she whispered.

"No, a series of tests are conducted to screen for kidney function, liver function, and viruses or infections like hepatitis. In addition, a urine specimen to check kidney function is necessary, a chest X-ray, and an electrocardiogram to ensure your heart and lungs are normal. Countless other tests could be required depending on the outcome. It's complicated, but thorough for the sake of the recipient *and* the donor."

She let out a long sigh.

"Agreeable donors also have to consult with their doctors about the final studies and a computerized tomography or CT scan has to be done."

"At least I've heard that term."

"Look, I admire your compassion, but the bottom line is … we're out of time."

She turned to face him, fear visible in her eyes. "I'll do whatever God gives me the ability. We can't give up, I won't hear of it!"

"Woman, you have the tenacity of mule—but for all the right reasons." He took her hands. "I admire those traits because I'm guilty of the same dogged determination."

"Frank and I won't leave this hospital until Loretta is in the clear."

"If I've learned anything at all, Terri Neal, I know you are steadfast when it comes to loyalty. I need to check on our patient. Will you stay in my office and rest until I return? Frank's in the waiting room, and I'll tell him where you are. After the surgery, and things calm down, I promise we *will* discuss whatever else is bothering you, okay?"

She nodded.

He kissed her lightly on the lips, gathered some paperwork off the desk, and left.

◆◆◆◆

Wade and Frank talked outside the intensive care unit while Weston paced in front of the double window. "Where'd you say Lou, or rather, *Terri* went?"

"Dr. Abraham took her to his office. The headstrong ninny demanded to be tested as a donor for the kidney transplant." Frank sighed.

"Me and Weston got a first class, up close and personal, taste of her stubbornness. She's as bad as Mom."

Tucker approached, dressed for surgery. "Hello Frank. Gentlemen, are you Ms. Carter's stepsons?"

"We don't use the term *stepson*. She's our mother — period," Wade's voice defiant.

"Sorry, didn't mean to offend anyone. I need to let you know what's going to happen," Tucker replied.

"About time somebody gave us some real information, and where is Lou, or Terri, or whatever the devil she calls herself? Did she run off and hide?" Weston stood nose to nose with the doctor.

"Ms. Neal is resting in my office. This is very traumatic for her, too. I think you should know, she requested to be a donor."

"Yeah, yeah, Frank already told us. Some nurse took blood from me and my brother, but wouldn't give us any details. What's the hell's going on?" Wade snarled.

Frank stepped in between the men. "Guys, this is hard on everyone. Let's listen to what the man has to say."

"As commendable as Terri's request is, we don't have time to go through all the preliminaries. The good news is we have located a viable donor, and I have a special internal surgeon in flight as we speak. We'll take your mother to surgery very soon. If you like, the two of you can go into ICU for a few minutes. However, don't be alarmed if she doesn't respond. It's a side effect of the heavy medication."

"Ya got her all doped up? Is that what you're trying to say?" Weston added.

"Trust me, Mr. Carter. This is a normal procedure for someone who has been through the trauma she suffered. The best scenario is for her to remain in a calm state and all vitals under control. As I said, you're welcome to visit briefly with your mother before we start surgery. She's in the fourth room on the right."

After the boys were out of sight, Tucker shuffled Frank around the corner. "Do you know any of these people?"

"No, I just met them a little while ago. Why do you ask?" Frank frowned.

"I had them do blood work on Terri, mainly to appease her request. The test results are back," Tucker whispered.

"And?"

"Its private information, but I think it might be in everyone's best interest if you were in the room when I talk to Terri, all right?"

"Of course. Is she okay? Please tell me she ain't sick or something. Don't pile more on me, Doc. I'm an old man," his voice wavered.

CHAPTER TWENTY EIGHT

A cannonade of thunder rumbled, and Terri opened her eyes unsure of the surroundings. Short breaths filled her lungs, and her heart hammered. Sallow light from the lamp on Tucker's desk cast an eerie glow. She sat upright on the brown leather couch and stared at the Grandfather clock in the corner pulsating to a metronome cadence. *How stupid of me. I slept for over an hour.* Panic surged. *I wanted to see Loretta before the surgery began.*

A creak of the doorknob, and she bolted to her feet. "Who, who's there?"

Someone flipped the light.

"Tucker, is that you?"

"Yes, are you okay?" He entered the office, a chart, and folders in hand.

"Surgery … is, is Mom in surgery? Did I miss my chance to talk to her?" The words came in spurts.

"It started over an hour ago."

"No, no, no. I needed to talk to her," she moaned.

"Sweetheart, I doubt she would have remembered any conversation. The pre-medication makes everyone groggy. Listen, it'll be a while, but after she comes out of recovery, there will be time to visit. Frank introduced me to Wade and Weston, and they are equally anxious." He laid the paperwork on the desk. "Both of them asked where you are. They want to see you."

"What if, what if she is mad and doesn't ever want to speak to me again? Are the twins mad? Do they blame me? Of course, they blame me—it's my fault." Both hands covered her face.

Tucker took a seat on the couch and pulled her down beside him. "Stop this garbage. No one blames you. The driver of the big truck who tried to beat a red light caused this mess, not you. The boys aren't angry, perhaps confused, but not mad." Arms cradled her close. "I have a few questions though. Why did you leave town, and who is Lou? I had something important to tell you, someone for you to meet. I called Frank a dozen times. After I couldn't locate you, I started to worry for your safety. After all, someone shot Frank."

Terri turned sideways on the cushion. "It is a long, stupid story. Are you sure you want to listen to such nonsense?"

A finger gently touched her cheek. "If it has to do with you, I'm always interested."

She glanced at the ceiling then back at the doctor. "Lou is the name I used when I introduced myself to Mom and the twins. Honestly, I never thought I'd see any of them again. These horrible circumstances wouldn't have happened if only I'd confronted you in the hospital. Instead, I tucked tail and ran off to Mom with my worry and woes. Somewhere in my pea brain, I decided if *I* couldn't find true love, perhaps Frank and Loretta would. Now, if they do ever meet, what if she despises him because of the misery I caused?"

"Wait, now *I'm* confused. You left because of what?" His eyes widened.

"Because I saw you with … her. I thought we had something special. Hell, I thought *I* was special. I'm a confident, content woman in most areas of my life, but I let down a wall, allowed you in my heart and my bed. Now, the realization is all the things you said were a devious guise. Guess you had a big laugh—at my expense. Those damn blue eyes drew me like a hypnotized moth to a flame, only to find out you're cruel and deceitful. Why, Tucker? It's apparent you can have any nurse in this hospital. Why hurt me?"

He tried to hold her arms as she continued to rave. "Terri, what do you mean?"

"The truth—I don't jump in bed with every man I date. How dare you take advantage of me? You liar!" Eye on the enemy, she wrestled free and stood.

"Whoa, who and what are you talking about?"

The words roared as she took a step back. "At least keep your dignity, man-up. I needed you, needed your help. I came to talk about Frank. He's involved in something bad, but you held another woman, planned to meet at six o'clock for a date."

He ran a hand through his hair. "I swear, Terri, there is no one else. You're the only one I've asked out in over a year. There aren't even any outside hobbies. All I did was work, until you walked into my life. Now, your face, your voice, fills my every waking thought. I've memorized every smile, every giggle, and all your mannerisms because I can't get enough of you."

"Don't lie to me. I heard you call her name … Nurse McKenzie."

A hand clamped over his mouth, and he gasped. "Oh my God, you are right." Slowly, he walked to the desk, reached over a large stack of files, and picked up a gold picture frame. "Did the woman look like this?" He thrust it forward.

"At least you've mustered some admission of guilt. I can't believe you actually have her photo on your desk, yet stood there and denied she existed."

Taste of Fire

His head twisted to the side as her hand slapped his face and a left a crimson imprint.

Except for the constant tempo of the old clock, silence filled the large office.

Tucker leaned against the desk, the picture still extended. "Would you do me one favor? Stop being so myopic, and please read what is written on this."

The frame broke and glass shattered like sparkling rhinestones as she yanked it away and hurled the picture against the wall.

"That is what I think of your Nurse McKenzie," she screamed.

"Listen to me, right now." His eyes glared and arms held her tight.

"Don't tell me what to …"

In an instant, his mouth found hers in a firm kiss.

Her pulse skittered as the embrace encompassed more of her body. She threw her arms around his neck, weak at the touch. Her mind relived their euphoric moments together "Stop, stop," she gasped. "Don't do this to me."

"Terri, I could never hurt you—I love you. When are you going to marry me?"

Silent breaths grew louder as their lips met in savage harmony.

He lifted her in his arms, plopped down on the couch, and cradled her in his lap.

"Listen to me. *McKenzie* Abraham is my sister. She came up here the other day to make sure I attended graduation. Makes me proud to say, she followed my example. I wanted you to be my date at Cordell University of Nursing over on Barber Drive when she walked the stage and received the diploma. The ceremony was at six o'clock, and I did call her *Nurse*

McKenzie. If you'd looked at the photo before you trashed it, you'd seen she signed it: 'With love, to the best big brother in the world'."

Face in the crook of his neck, she blubbered, "Your … your sister?"

Tucker stood, slid Terri onto the couch, and got down on one knee. "Geez, this is not how I practiced it in my head, but here goes. I love you, Firefighter Neal. Maybe it's a little premature because I don't have a ring, but I pledge my love to you, now and forever. Will you marry me?"

Taste of Fire
CHAPTER TWENTY NINE

The tyrant thunderstorm passed, and night descended. A constant flow of nurses, orderlies, and doctors traveled the hall on the ICU floor. Frank pushed up off the hard cushion in the waiting room and let out a small groan. *My old back is stiff as a board. I need to move around.* He glanced at the twins.

Wade lay stretched out on a nearby couch, the pewter-colored Stetson over his face. Weston used a magazine to shield the light in a makeshift bed of two chairs.

Grateful Tucker convinced Terri to rest in his office, Frank headed to the nurses' station. *Maybe I can sweet talk one of those ladies into a hot cup of coffee.*

Loretta Carter was out of surgery, but still in recovery. So many unanswered questions continued to rob Frank of rest. *She must be something special for Little T to be so enchanted.* He shook his head. *What an awesome first date this turned out to be.*

A ward clerk directed him to an area with fresh brewed coffee and juice. He returned, cup in hand, to find the twins still asleep.

They appeared to be fine young men. One thing for certain, they loved their stepmother. Earlier, he listened to stories of how their biological mother fought a brave battle against breast cancer. The longsuffering left their dad lost, lonesome, and depressed. Alcohol served as a distraction for the man, a hopeless avenue to overcome grief. After the excessive, destructive behavior erupted in a drunken altercation with a loyal ranch hand, the twins forced him to seek professional help.

Taste of Fire

At an AA meeting, Waymon Carter met Loretta, a recovering alcoholic, who volunteered time to help others facing the constant arduous fight. The boys said she brought light and love back into all of their cold empty lives. They idolized her.

The cell phone buzzed in Frank's pocket, and the number on caller ID made him shudder. Coffee sloshed over the edge of the cup. "Yeah, what do you want?"

"Hey buddy, you don't sound too happy to hear from me," a snippy voice replied.

"I'm at the hospital, can't really talk." He headed away from the twins to speak in private.

"Hospital? You gettin' to like that place? Well, play nice, and maybe I won't send you back. I need more money, and I need it in a hurry. When you gonna send another payment?" Orin snarled.

Frank took a sip of the hot liquid and paced back and forth. *God help me; I might not live through another surly confrontation.* "Man, give me a little time, please."

He caught a glimpse of Tucker entering the waiting room. "Look, I'll get it soon as I can, but I gotta go. There's a doctor walking up." A click on the cell phone, and the conversation died. Braced against the wall, Frank attempted to calm the nerves. After a little prayer, he headed back to the twins.

Weston ran a hand through his hair. "Your doctor friend just left. Everything went good with the transplant, and Mom's vitals are normal. He also said we could see her at the next visiting hour."

"Well, that *is* good news, guys." Frank smiled.

Wade rubbed the brim of the cowboy hat. "Yeah, tell me something. This Dr. Abraham, is he the joker Terri got so upset about and came to talk to Mom?"

"Well, they have dated." Frank sat the cup on an end table. "I really don't know about their personal problems, if there are any. I thought she came to see your mother because of me." He chuckled.

"Oh, she definitely wanted the two of you to meet, but when she got to Skirts and Spurs that night there was some kind of burr under her saddle. She and Mom did the girl-talking thing later at our house. Me and Weston went to bed, and I could hear them laughing. A few hours later, I woke up thirsty and headed to the kitchen. My bedroom is next to the guestroom where Terri slept. I thought I heard her crying. Hey, it ain't none of my business other than ..." he paused.

"Other than, he was starting to like the woman," Weston interjected.

"As a matter of fact, I think both you boys are pretty cute," a female voice chimed.

"And what about me?" Frank pretended to pout.

"Well, you are taken, that is, as soon as Loretta can meet you. Trust me, she'll want you all to herself." Terri hugged Frank.

◆◆◆◆

Hues of peach and blue water-colored the Alabama sky as Frank pulled into the Griffin County Hospital parking lot. The sinking sun cast soft shadows on the front of the building. Terri asked him to meet her and Tucker to talk. *Little T insists on playing cupid. The twins said Loretta is in a private room now. Heck, this woman needs to rest. It's only been a few days. No sense to worry 'bout some dumb date.* A flutter in his stomach made him shiver. *Jiminy, I'm too dang old to be nervous.*

The elevator door opened, and Terri and Tucker stood in the hall.

Frank threw up a hand. "Hey there, everything okay? Where are the boys?"

"I let them have the first part of the visit to see their mother. Even though she is in a private room, it's still ICU. We can go in for the last part. Right now, Tucker and I have to talk to you privately," Terri said.

"Sure."

The threesome travelled down the elevator to Tucker's office.

"What's all this hush-hush stuff? Couldn't we talk in the waiting area?" Frank scratched his head.

"I suppose, but this is personal, very personal," Tucker began. "I intended to have this conversation a few days ago. If you remember, I asked you to be in the room with Terri."

"Yup, but you left," Frank replied.

"Yes, they paged me and things got busy on another floor. Anyway, we both know Terri's insistence as a kidney donor. I pacified her by doing blood work, although I knew I couldn't let her go through with the surgery if there was an available donor."

"Fortunately, you found one. I know all that, Doc." Frank eased down on the couch to rest the gimpy knee.

"I ordered a barrage of tests. For some strange reason, I felt compelled to take it a step further, and believe me, the results are unbelievable." Tucker leafed through a stack of papers.

In a nearby chair, Terri sat silent, an awkward expression on her face.

"Little T, what's he trying to say? Are you okay? That's all I want to know. Dear God, please tell me you're all right."

"Frank ..." Terri whispered. "Frank, she is my ... my *mother*."

"What?" The older man gasped.

"The DNA remarks on Terri's information are a perfect match to Loretta Carter's." Tucker walked over to Frank and offered a chart. "See how each line up perfect?"

"Then, that woman in the hospital room, the woman you wanted me to meet, the woman who is the stepmother to those two boys, Wade and Weston, is *her* biological mother?" Frank's body crumpled in a heap. Blackness shrouded the room, and he felt weightless. Words wouldn't form, and light evaded his vision.

"He's opening his eyes now. I think he'll be okay."

A faint voice in the distance sounded like Tucker, but Frank wasn't sure. *What happened? Where, where am I?* A putrid, sharp odor permeated his nostrils. A gurgle formed in his throat, and he struggled to focus.

Terri dabbed a wet cloth. "Please, open your eyes. Talk to me, Frank, please."

"Huh? What're you doing?" He swallowed hard. "Get that silly rag off my face. I'm fine."

"You passed out, and I grabbed some smelling salts," Tucker replied.

"Don't tell me I fainted like a dang ol' sissy girl," the man grumbled.

Terri and Tucker laughed.

"We're afraid so. It's good to see you still have a sense of humor though," she added.

"Why you passed out has me concerned," Tucker replied.

"For pity's sake, once a doctor always a doctor. Help me sit up. The old knee is a booger today." He grunted as they aided him to an upright position. "Ain't nuthin' wrong except—if that woman is Terri's mother, there's a whole lot more to this story than anyone can imagine."

♦♦♦

The hospital corridor seemed stuffy as if all the oxygen was squeezed from the air. Terri tried to remain calm as the threesome neared Loretta's room. In one hand, she held the clear plastic bag of personal items Tucker gave her the day of the accident.

A few feet from the doorway, Tucker touched her elbow. "Neither of us wants to interfere, but this is a monumental moment for you. I'd be glad stand by your side if you like."

She looked into his cobalt eyes and saw truth, compassion. "Thanks, but I need to do this on my own, just don't be too far away, okay? You, too, Frank."

Both men nodded.

"We'll be right outside the door, Little T."

The overhead light cast a gray shadow across the hospital bed. The bandages on Loretta's face gave the image of a semi-mummy. Fuchsia and violet contusions tinted her skin. A formation of monitors and tubes recorded each vital sign and beeped in a high pitch chorus.

Terri approached, almost afraid to breath. The small plastic bag felt heavy and cumbersome. Trembling, she took Loretta's hand.

No response.

A cold emptiness jarred the pit of her stomach. Head bowed, she stared at the sterile white sheet.

A strong arm caressed her shoulder. "Sorry, I just couldn't let you do this alone," Tucker said.

"I'm scared."

"Don't worry. I promise, everything is fine. The meds make her unresponsive."

169

TASTE OF FIRE

Loretta coughed and slowly opened her eyes. "Who's unresponsive?"

"Oh Mom, don't try to talk, rest. Go back to sleep, please," Terri begged.

"Lord have mercy, I can sleep when I'm dead and buried in the ground. It isn't every day I wake up to see an angel and a handsome doctor."

"Ms. Carter, you're right. This girl *is* an angel." Tucker pulled Terri close.

"Mom, I have your things." She offered the bag. "But the necklace—where did you get it?"

"Wha ... what?"

"Where? Where did you get it? Tell me," Terri's voice elevated.

"Sweetheart, what are you doing?" Tucker intervened.

She ripped open the plastic. "Where's the other half? Where?" In her hand, a silver chain with half a heart dangled.

"I've had it a long time." Loretta cleared her throat. "Just an old necklace I always wear."

"No. It's a piece to *my* past. Who gave it to you? Tell me?"

Frank stepped up to the bed. "Loretta?"

Silence pierced the room.

Loretta turned toward the doorway. "Oh my God, it's you, Frank. It's you," she wailed. Her body went limp as she lost consciousness. The beepers started to squeal in alarm.

"Clear the room, both of you," Tucker demanded.

CHAPTER THIRTY

A blend of aromas from the food-laden table filled Terri's dining room. "Does anyone need more coffee or tea?" She placed a hand on Loretta's shoulder.

"No sweetheart, please sit down. Don't make such a fuss. You've already been generous enough by letting me and the boys stay here while I recover."

"Heck, I thought Mom's cooking couldn't be beat, but I think there might be a new chef in town." Weston rubbed his stomach.

"Yeah well, you could've left a little roast for the rest of us, you hog." Wade waved the fork like a sword at his brother. "How many servings did you have?"

"My favorite was those scalloped potatoes, Little T. Gotta confess, I took a double helping. I ate grass and all." Frank wiped his mouth on the linen napkin.

"Grass? I garnished the potatoes with parsley, silly." She laughed and returned to the chair next to Tucker.

"Yup, looks like I'll be on a diet before long." He winked and stood as she sat down.

"Good gravy, I have to cook at the Station House, so I'm not a stranger to a frying pan, you guys." Terri rolled her eyes. "It is nice to have everyone here and healthy, though. Most of all, it's the least I could do." She turned to Loretta. "Please, let me apologize again for my stupid explosion in the hospital."

"Nonsense, you couldn't help but react to such an unexpected situation." Loretta smiled.

"There's no good excuse for my behavior. You were still in ICU and barely out of recovery."

"Shush, child. I've already forgotten it." The older woman took a sip of sweet tea.

"If you feel okay, would you please finish the story?" Seated between Frank and Tucker, Terri took each by the hand.

A long sigh escaped from Loretta's lips. "Of course. After all, they say confession is good for the soul." She refolded the napkin in her lap. "When I married Charles Terrance 'Chuck' Neal, I was pregnant. He knew, but never asked about the father. Idle tongues around town hurled vicious gossip at him, but he always smiled, never once denied it. For some reason, he loved me, obviously more than I ever deserved. We made an appointment at the Justice of the Peace in the next county to perform the ceremony. Your daddy insisted I have a new outfit, so we went to a little bridal shop. I'll never forget the dress, a beige suit with lace lapels. One of the nicest I'd ever owned. Chuck carried on as if I was some famous runway model. When the storeowner found out our plan to *elope*, she gave me a beautiful bouquet of yellow silk roses."

Loretta paused and took another drink of tea. "Chuck also knew I was prone to take a nip from time to time. Never did like the taste, but guilt drove the desire to drink. In my irrational mind, it provided an escape. When it escalated during the pregnancy, he scolded me, and rightly so. Believe me; it was not to harm the baby. Every day, I told myself I could change and beat the demons, but not so." Tears filled her eyes.

"God is good. You were born alive, normal, and healthy. While I breast-fed, I didn't touch the stuff, but my milk didn't satisfy you. The doctor suggested we try some formula." She shook her head. "Didn't take long to fall back into those toxic old ways. I hid it, or so I thought, but Chuck always knew, and his patience grew weary. We argued so much over the issue. He begged me to get help, said he'd even go along. How could a man like him love me so much? In my silly brain, I didn't deserve to be loved by anyone … a woman so jaded, unworthy, which made the battle harder. The fights became more frequent." She pushed back from the table.

"One night while he worked graveyard shift, I got really soused and threw up all over the nursery floor before I could reach the bathroom. At the sink, I caught my reflection in the mirror, dark circles under my eyes, face gaunt, and pale. Thick steam filled the room as I stood under the hot shower spray in an attempt to wash away the heartache from my mistakes. Right there, I vowed to tell my husband the truth—the name of the biological father." She turned to Frank.

He sat up straight.

"Is, is Little T mine? She *is* my little girl, isn't she?" His eyes widened as the words tumbled out.

Terri felt his grip tighten on her hand.

"I've always loved you, Loretta, always."

"Frank, I loved you back then, too, but couldn't stand some of those rough thugs in your circle of friends. Then you disappeared without a word. Talk around town was you went into the service. Others laughed and said jail. I felt like the brunt of a bad joke, betrayed and belittled. To me, there weren't any two better men in the state of Alabama than Frank Gunnison and Chuck Neal, best friends since their teens. Guess I flirted enough to turn Chuck's head and my vindication came in the way of a marriage proposal." She looked down. "Sweet child, the scar you bear is my fault."

Terri ran a hand over the sleeved-covered arm.

TASTE OF FIRE

Elbows on the table, hands clasped, Loretta began again, "The day of the wreck, I had been drinking—drinking because Orin Chambers came to the house."

"What?" Frank choked.

"This is very hard to tell because I kept it buried for so long, but I'm glad to be free of the anger and pain." Tears poured. "My baby girl and I watched purple thunderhead clouds float across a glorious sunset that spring evening. We had a mason jar ready to catch fireflies when a car pulled in the drive. Orin got out, wanted to talk to my ol' man'. When I said Chuck was at work, he let out a hideous laugh. I'll never forget the malevolent look in his eyes like a wild animal. Without warning, he grabbed me around the waist. His breath reeked of whiskey and cigarettes." Her hands covered her face.

"I had on a pair of shorts and a tee shirt. Before I could react, he threw me in the back seat of the car and jerked down the shorts. Thunder rolled as a storm approached, and I tried to scream, but he said if I did my little girl would be next."

"Oh God, Loretta!" Frank cried.

"The only good thing was the buzz, from the alcohol I drank earlier, seemed to numb the reality of the act." She paused. "I remember worrying if Terri would wander out of the yard after the blinking little bugs. How I prayed to God those little eyes didn't see the evilness." She sobbed.

"After he finished, he pushed me out onto the ground and let out another guttural laugh. On hands and knees, I crawled to my baby, threw her on my hip, and ran inside. We had to get away. I managed to grab your favorite teddy bear off the floor and a bottle from the fridge."

Taste of Fire

"My, my teddy bear? The raggedy one in your guestroom where I slept?" Terri looked stunned.

"Yes, the very same one. A few moments later, the front door slammed behind me, and I knew it was him. I ran out the back. It was dark by then, and rain was pouring down. The key jammed in the ignition, and I couldn't get the car to start. Thank the Lord, just as he slapped the window and growled for me to open the door the motor turned over."

Terri handed Loretta a box of tissue as she wiped away her own tears.

Frank sat motionless like a stone statue, gaze fixed on the woman.

"Between fear, rain-slick roads, and the booze, I lost control of the car. The wreck was bad. The car caught on fire. Now, you know the whole truth about the scar. Chuck never forgave me. He loved Terri as his own. I should've told him the story about Chambers raping me, but I knew he would kill the man. Enough mistakes were already made. I didn't want to ruin another life. He went to a divorce lawyer and started the proceedings, as well as filed a permanent injunction against me so I ... I could never see you."

Terri ran to Loretta.

"Understand honey, I left on my own, but I always loved my baby girl. I swore to get my life straight. Regardless, you were better off with Chuck, not me."

"Where in blazes is this Orin character, now? Wade pushed back his chair and went to Loretta's side.

"We'll hunt him down, Mom—make him pay." Weston joined the group.

Tucker stood, hands raised. "Look everyone, the past is gone. Why not look forward to the future? We're all fortunate to have one another."

"You're right, Doc. Ain't gonna change things, anyway. That ol' scumbag, Orin Chambers, is a dead-end road," Frank replied. "I don't mean to sound disrespectful, Loretta.

"No, I agree." She put an arm around the twins. "God brought these two wonderful men in my life, and I'm blessed. Last thing I need is for something to happen to one of them or Terri. Let's all sit back down."

"Mom, what about your niece and your sister?" Terri asked.

"Honey, when we talked the other night, I made up the story. The boys are my only family … until now."

"Excuse me." Terri disappeared down the hall.

Tucker stood and pushed the chair back from the table.

"Let her go, Doc," Frank said.

"This is so much to take in. I just worry about her," he replied.

A few moments later, she returned with a small oak box in one hand and a torn plastic bag in the other.

"So, you actually are my birth mother?" Terri pulled a crinkled photo from the coffer and handed it to Loretta.

"Goodness gracious, that's me years ago."

"And the necklace—what does it mean?" Terri fondled the piece of jewelry.

"Oh my gosh, the other half heart." Loretta's eyes widened. "When you put them together it reads, **My Love I Give My Heart To You.**"

"Uh, the one you saw in the plastic bag at the hospital musta been the one I gave her years ago," Frank confessed.

"If that's true, how did Daddy end up with this half?"

"We all have some skeletons, and I guess it's my turn." Frank shook his head. "I lost it to Chuck in a poker game. I use to join the guys at the Station House for their weekly card night. I'd drank a lot of beer and decided to have a little pity party over old memories. Stupid me boasted I'd beat 'em all, even put up the deed on the Short Cut. Chuck shot it down, asked about the chain around my neck. After a quick yank, I slid the dang thing across the table at him. Maybe he always knew Loretta had the other half. I don't know. He took it in place of the deed." Shoulders slumped, he continued, "Something else, I never went to Viet Nam."

Terri frowned. "But the busted knee, your limp, there's a scar …"

"Lies — I made it all up, sorry. See, Orin Chambers talked me into going for a ride in a souped-up car one night. Heck, I didn't have a clue he boosted it."

"Wait a dang minute. You are friends with this Orin monster?" Weston pointed a finger.

"Son, we were all young and stupid back then, lived life in the moment, I suppose. The short story is we got caught, or rather, *I* got caught. Orin bolted into the forest and left me behind. The sheriff charged me as an accomplice and hauled my butt to prison. My story, they discharged me from the service because of an injury, was the best explanation I could conjure up. Everyone loves a hero. Truth is, I was a zero and too ashamed to tell my friends I'd been in jail." He turned to Terri. "Except for Chuck … I told him the truth only a few weeks before he died."

A hand rubbed the injured knee. "This resulted from a whippin' out on the prison yard by some of Orin's 'inside' friends. After I got back into town, and heard Loretta married Chuck, all hope of a life with my only true love dissolved. I figured you were *his* baby girl." He started to cry. "I would have married you Loretta, but I didn't know."

"This explains why I qualified to give Loretta a kidney," Terri's voice trembled.

"The blood work I requested provided the DNA information," Tucker interjected. "I only tried to be thorough to make you happy."

"So, you put the pieces of my life puzzle together." Terri stood and paced back and forth. "If my daddy loved me as much as everyone claims, why couldn't he be honest? Oh, he gave me an explanation, but I grew up thinking my mother abandoned me *and* him."

"Sweetheart, he raised you by himself, did a blasted fine job of it, too," Frank said. "Perhaps in his mind, it sheltered an innocent victim from the unspeakable truth."

"Terri, I always loved you, but never believed I deserved any in return. I gave life to you, and with your help you gave me this." Loretta clutched her side.

"Guess we'll always share these scars of life." Terri kissed Loretta's cheek.

"Yes we will my beautiful daughter, yes we will."

The two women stood to embrace one another.

"But my biological father?"

Loretta gestured toward Frank. "That man right there."

Hands over his face, Frank wept aloud. The women went to him.

"How did I ever get so lucky to have both of you?" He sniffed.

"Hey, it's a package deal, *Dad*," Weston teased.

"Yup, I'd say you just doubled your trouble with the likes of taking on all of us. Good luck." Wade stuck out a hand to Frank.

"Well, looks like a party is in order," Tucker replied. "Frank, you not only have a daughter, but you might even get a wife and two stepsons out of the deal."

"What? I have a sister now?" Weston chuckled.

"Guess that sort of takes care of my wanting to date you, doesn't it?" Wade grinned.

"On the idea of dating, I'll have a say." Tucker took Terri by the hand. "You see, I asked her to marry me the day of the transplant." He paused. "I'm pleased to say she accepted. So Frank, add a son-in-law to your family tree."

"Doggit, I was hoping Terri would get rid of my brother for me." Weston sighed.

"Hey, come to think of it, I have a couple of sisters you might want to meet." Tucker rubbed his chin.

"Yes, I've seen one of them, and she's gorgeous." Terri winked.

Taste of Fire
CHAPTER THIRTY ONE

The revelation of long hidden secrets and confessions from the past birthed new emotions as Terri skirted around the kitchen. The buzz from a houseful of people filled the little bungalow Chuck Neal built, and it finally seemed like a real home. Growing up, with only one parent and no siblings, often made it seem empty. Damp dishtowel in hand, she reflected on the pleasure of houseguests.

Although a bit resistant, Loretta agreed to stay in Terri's bedroom to recuperate. Weston took the extra room, and Wade bunked on the couch where LC curled at his feet.

Terri slept in the alcove of the attic, a favorite hideaway place. As a child, she loved to visit the make-believe family who resided there. The handsome father worked and made lots of money. Of course, the beautiful mother adored all the children, and there were many, but most of all she loved the dark-haired girl named *Terri*.

Plates clattered as Tucker filled the dishwasher, and the reverie dissolved. "Will you always be so eager to help?" She took a canister of coffee out of the cabinet.

"After we're married? Of course." He leaned against the counter.

"Our schedules will be outrageous at times." She walked to his side. "Do you think you can handle KP duty alone?"

Arms around her waist, he kissed her softly. "Sure. Didn't I tell you, I can make a mean bowl of soup?"

"Is that right?" She giggled. "What about baby bottles?"

An eyebrow cocked. "Oh I see. This is a trick question. I'll have you know, I practically raised my sisters, McKenzie and Sheridan. So, when the time comes bring on the diapers, formula, or bottles—I'm ready. I shall forever profess my amaranthine love for you."

She put her arms around his neck. "It's so sexy when you use big words."

His mouth captured hers, and they lingered in a passionate kiss.

"If that does the trick, let me rattle off some more. I have lots of medical terms that are sensual sounding like zoonosis or scarlatina." He nuzzled her neck.

"You probably, uh think, I don't, uh … even know what that means, but one has to do with animals and uh, the other is, uh … scarlet fever." She took in little breaths as the embrace became more licentious, each movement quixotic.

A loud cackle of laughter from the front room shattered the impromptu tryst.

Terri straightened the rumpled blouse and ran a hand through her hair. "Since, Frank played cupid, will he be your best man?"

"Sounds good to me." They kissed once more. "Look sweetheart, sorry I got carried away, but I'm so in love with you. It's difficult to stay in control sometimes. You're all I think about … and not only for moments like that, although, they are very special."

"I feel the same way."

He grabbed her up, whirled around the kitchen, and set her back down. "Guess we better join the group before I carry you upstairs. Since you said Loretta is occupying your room for a while, she might not appreciate a bunch of wrinkled bedcovers."

Taste of Fire

Hand in hand, they returned to living room.

Conversations continued, tears flowed, and hilarity filled the house.

"I need to see if the fresh pot of coffee is ready. Excuse me." Terri headed to the kitchen.

As she passed through the dining room, Frank's cell phone lay on the table. Seconds later, the familiar melodious tune chimed. "Frank? Frank, get your phone." On the third ring, she set the pot of coffee down and sprinted to the table. *Dang, it went to voice mail.*

Out of curiosity, she checked the caller ID. Goosebumps formed. *Orin Chambers? Why in the world would such a demonic person have Frank's number now?* Lightheaded, the phone fell from her hand. *My God, Frank could be in trouble. I have to tell Tucker.* Loretta and Frank's stories, still raw in her mind, she bolstered strength to join the crowd.

"Uh, I need to run to the store for a couple of items. Tucker, would you take me?" A forced smile appeared. "We'll be right back. Please, everyone continue to make yourself at home. Coffee is on the counter and blueberry muffins in a covered basket for dessert."

Weston let out a grunt. "I'm stuffed, but blueberry muffins are my weakness."

"Food period is your weakness." Wade jumped in front of his brother. "Beat ya to the kitchen."

Inside Tucker's SUV, Terri grabbed his arm. "We have to talk, and this cannot go any further than this vehicle. Do you understand?"

"Your hand is cold as ice. Are you okay? What's going on, baby?"

"Pull onto the street. I don't want anyone to get suspicious." The seat belt snapped shut.

Taste of Fire

A couple blocks away, she explained in detail the night of the altercation with the arrogant intruder at the Short Cut.

The blinker clicked as Tucker turned onto the main highway. "I read in the newspaper about the incident. The article said Sergeant Parker arrested the thug. What does it have to do with anything?"

"Less than a week later, Frank was shot," her voice rose. "Of course, he told everyone he was mugged and some ridiculous garbage about going back inside to check on a stupid mop. Frank isn't careless, sweetheart. I think it was the same jerk, and I also think he intended to kill Frank."

"Have you voiced these concerns to Sergeant Green?"

"No, but wouldn't you think he'd put this together? After all, he responded to the call when I decked the guy—even ribbed me about it."

At the next red light, he turned to Terri. "Want me to stop at the grocery store two blocks up?" In the parking lot, he cut off the engine. "I sense there's more. We didn't really need to come here, did we?"

Elbow propped on the armrest, she began, "The reason I came to the hospital to talk to you that day was because of Frank. It's a long story, but I tracked him down at a pawnshop over in Raunch."

"Good grief, Terri. You went there alone? For pity's sake, it's a dangerous, rough part of town. We get gunshot victims and domestic violence cases in the emergency room all the time from there. It isn't safe. I hear the pimps cruise the streets day and night to keep tabs on the girls working every corner." He shook his head.

"Please, please don't lecture me. Because it appeared you had a new girlfriend, I went to cry on Frank's shoulder. He passed me going the opposite direction; didn't wave or speak. Naturally, I followed to see where he was headed in such a hurry."

"What did he say? What did you find out? Did he meet this Orin Chambers fellow?"

"Well, he went to a sleazy pawn shop."

"How do you know?"

"Because, I waited around the corner until he left the place then I went inside. He hocked his most prized possession—his grandfather's antique pocket watch. The guy behind the bulletproof glass …"

"Bulletproof glass? Terri, you could've been mugged or worse. Promise me you'll never do anything so dangerous again without me."

"Guess I was more afraid of *not* knowing. It's isn't my everyday practice to traipse around on the wrong side of town by myself, but Frank is family. After a little finagling with the owner, I bought the watch. Frank doesn't even know."

"We could confront him privately later tonight. There's probably a logical explanation. Maybe he needed money. The club was out of commission for a while. Could've been a simple cash flow problem."

"Perhaps, but this is minor compared to what I learned a little while ago at the house," she continued.

"At the house?" An eyebrow rose. "I heard the same stories as you."

"Yes, but when I got up to check on the coffee, Frank's cell phone was on the dining room table and started to ring. I called out for him to answer, but everyone was talking and laughing. I picked it up just as it went to voice mail. Something made me look at the caller ID." She paused. "The name that came up was Orin Chambers.

"So, you think this shady character might be the one who mugged Frank?"

"There's nothing to prove my theory, but after Loretta explained the rape incident, it makes me wonder. Doesn't it you?"

"Well, Frank and Orin go way back. Do you think he knows Loretta is in town? Terri, if that's the case, you could be in more danger than Frank. After all, you put the jerk in jail."

"I jacked him up one time, I can do it …"

Tucker placed a finger to her lips. "Don't even go there. Yeah, you're stronger than most women are physically and emotionally which I find pretty sexy. However, this guy is a hardened criminal, a brute who hides behind the coattails of others and doesn't care if there's a fall guy. Whether or not he's been in jail doesn't matter. There's no way I'm going to let him harm you. Hear me?"

A hand flew to her mouth. "What if, after the deal at the Short Cut, he threatened to hurt me in some way, and that's why Frank was shot?"

"We shouldn't speculate. Give Frank a chance to explain. If we aren't satisfied with his answer, then *together* we'll go see your cop friend."

Terri's eyes widened. "All I know is Orin Chambers tried to contact Frank."

Taste of Fire
CHAPTER THIRTY TWO

The sun cast a muted glare across the terra cotta and gray brick building of the Anniston Police Department. The United States and Alabama flags, sentinels in the landscaped courtyard, flapped in a brisk wind. In the side parking lot, a black and white patrol car eased to a halt. The sign above the designated spot read "Sergeant Green."

Parker stepped out of the cruiser, deep in thought. The shift started on the run, three domestic disturbance calls and two fender benders. Any other time, a fast pace fueled the daily adrenaline rush, but today something caviled at his mind as if an omen of evil lurked.

He glanced around the grounds, waist-high shrubbery, and metal-covered entry. Was it a premonition, gut feeling, or only sapient training? The car door slammed shut.

A triangular red, white, and blue emblem of an eagle and flag covered the building's back door. He punched in the code to enter as the miniature shoulder microphone crackled. "Central to 253; what's your 20?"

"253 to Central, I'm 10-7 at the station." The heavy metal door thudded shut. A cluster of keys from his hip jangled in the lock to the dispatch center. "You need me, Janie?"

A thin blonde in uniform looked up over several monitors and winked. "Hmm, is that a personal question, or did you want to know the reason why I paged you?"

Willow green eyes widened as he strutted closer. "Any time you want to go for a burger at the Short Cut just let me know."

Head tilted, she grinned. "Actually, there's a phone message." A yellow sticky note waved from manicured fingers.

Paper in hand, his tone changed, "Dr. Abraham wants to talk to *me*?"

The girl covered up the microphone. "You know, if you aren't feeling well I can always kiss it and make it all better." She turned away to respond to a request for a drivers license check.

"You sure know how to make my day, Janie."

As he left, he heard the reply, "What about your night?"

A couple doors down the long corridor, he entered an office occupied by two detectives, each leaned back, feet propped on the desk.

"Hey Fletch. You and Spence working hard, I see."

"Do I detect a tone of jealousy?" One man replied.

"The only thing you can detect is an easy pay check." Parker picked up a phone and dialed the number from the note.

A familiar voice answered, "This is Neal."

"Hey girl—thought I was calling Dr. Abraham. What's up? Is Frank okay?"

"Thanks for getting back to us so quick. Listen Parker, Tucker and I need to talk to you in private. Can you be at the hospital in about twenty minutes?"

Tucker? Wonder when they went to a first name basis? "Yeah, is something wrong?"

"Can't go into it on the phone. See ya in a bit." The phone clicked.

◆◆◆◆

The patrol called stopped at the side access of the Griffin County Hospital. At the nurses' station, Parker requested a page. It was only moments before a tall, familiar figure appeared, alone.

The two men shook hands.

"Where's Terri, and what's going on?"

"Hello, Sergeant Green. Let's go to my office." Tucker motioned. "I'll explain the situation."

They wove through a group of people to reach the elevator. On the second floor, Parker followed the doctor to a door near the end of hall.

"I appreciate your time, Sergeant."

"Sure, sure, now what's this about? I thought Terri wanted to speak to me." Parker sat down in one of the leather chairs in front of the mahogany desk.

"That was the intention. However, after Frank didn't answer his phone, she left." Tucker cleared some files on the desktop to sit on the edge.

"Should I go check on Frank, too?"

"Although there are some legitimate concerns, let's wait to hear from Terri. She promised to keep in touch."

The policeman settled back in the chair, but uneasiness lingered.

"Let me bring you up to-date on a few important items. Are you aware Terri requested to be a kidney donor for her friend, Loretta Carter—the woman involved in the accident at the intersection of Pilot Butte and Corey Drive?"

"What? Nope, but sounds like something that crazy girl would do."

Tucker chuckled. "A bit hard-headed, isn't she? I did find a transplant match for Ms. Carter, but not before Terri insisted on a gamut of tests to check compatibility. The results provided unexpected and startling information ... actually, life changing news."

Taste of Fire

"Is Terri sick? Is that why this is so secretive? Oh Lord, what's the diagnosis?" Parker fidgeted in the chair.

"Slow down, let me continue. Terri is fine. Thing is, she met the woman by coincidence on a recent out of town trip. Ms. Carter came to Anniston per Terri's request to meet Frank Gunnison. Seems the lady firefight decided to play matchmaker, thought the two would be perfect for one another. However, the accident put Loretta in the hospital."

"The activity board at the PD listed the wreck and the details. Alford and Cain worked it. They said Terri was at the scene, but I wasn't aware she knew the victim involved."

"Well, it is gets pretty bizarre." Tucker clasped his hands together. "The information I am about to divulge is strictly confidential. Even though she gave me permission to share it with you, we both would appreciate complete discretion, if you will."

"Of course, not a problem," Parker agreed.

The wheels of the executive chair squeaked as the doctor pulled it out and sat down behind the desk. "Loretta Carter and her twin stepsons, Wade and Weston, own a dance club outside of Atlanta. Apparently, patrons and friends call the lady Mom. The casual friendship became more of a bond after Terri needed another female to confide in. Therefore, she made a second trip. For whatever reason, and who knows how, she convinced the woman to come here, like I said to meet Frank. The girls traveled in separate vehicles and had just made it into town when the accident occurred."

"So, Frank doesn't know Ms. Carter?"

"In a manner of speaking, he didn't, but actually does." Tucker shook his head.

"Because Terri introduced them after the wreck, I guess."

"No, he knew Ms. Carter previously ... from the past."

The officer crossed his arms. "Now wait, you're talking in riddles."

"Trust me, Parker, this *is* a puzzle and gets much more complicated. Since Loretta's vehicle was behind Terri's when the truck barreled through the intersection, our girl is convinced it's her fault."

"Good grief. Is she headstrong or what?"

"You've known her longer than me. Glad it isn't just my opinion." Tucker grinned. "The tests I ordered to appease Terri also provided DNA markers. When the reports came back, the information was shocking. Loretta Carter, or Mom, is Terri's actual birth mother."

"Huh, uh what?"

"The Carters are guests at Terri's house while Loretta recuperates from the surgery. We all had dinner there last night, and as it turns out, Frank knew her even before Terri was born ... they were once in love."

"Okay, but obviously they didn't marry. So, how does Terri fit in?"

"Another piece to the puzzle. Did you know Terri's father?"

"Yeah, Terrance Neal, Captain at the fire department. Everybody called him Chuck. He passed away several years ago—had an awesome reputation. See, there's a healthy competition between cops and firefighters. We do community events like softball or golf tourneys. Whenever we'd have an

Emergency/Safety Expo, the man always whipped our butt in every exhibition. Terri took his death hard, but understandably so. A lot of guys say that's why she joined the force."

"Well, Mr. Neal married Loretta aware she was already pregnant."

"Again, how does Terri, fit in? I mean ..." Parker's brow furrowed. "Holy crap, are you telling me Frank is her father, not Chuck?"

"He volunteered to give blood for Loretta, and I decided to cross check it with the other DNA results." Tucker handed Parker a manila file.

"Look, don't take it the wrong way, but I don't need any proof. I just need to know how this involves me." The folder landed on the desk.

"I didn't ask you here to catch up on some soap opera. There's a real purpose to the meeting. Remember the guy Terri encountered at the Short Cut and your officers put in jail?"

"According to the report Paco Taliaferro filed, it was a creep named Orin Chambers. She did a real number on him, too." He snickered.

"The jerk happens to be a skeleton from Frank's past. I won't go into the details, but Terri has knowledge the guy called Frank yesterday. She can tell you more later, but the theory is he's the one who mugged and shot Mr. Gunnison."

"What?" Parker leaned forward, hands on the chair arms.

"*Ms. Detective* followed Frank to a pawn shop in Rauch," Tucker continued.

"Rauch? What the hell? When the PD responds to a call there, it is mandated backup. We can't go in alone. Has she lost her mind? Plus, why would the old guy take such a dangerous chance after his narrow escape at the Short Cut? Doesn't make sense." He rubbed a temple. "There's at least three or four hock stops on this side of town. Why venture over there?"

"Our best guess is to not be recognized. He pawned his grandfather's pocket watch, which Terri bought back. She said it had to be a desperate move on Frank's part. Our belief is Orin Chambers might be blackmailing Frank—perhaps to keep him quiet over the break in."

Adrenaline surged. "I've got to get back to the PD." Parker headed toward the door. "I need to go over something with one of our forensic guys."

"Wait. That isn't all. Loretta explained the reason she abandoned her husband and little girl was because this thug, Chambers, raped her. Shame and fear drove her to run the night he attacked her which resulted in a fiery car wreck." Tucker walked around the desk. "Have you ever seen the scar on Terri's arm?"

"Not first hand, but I've heard she's pretty spirited about it."

The ring of Tucker's cell phone disrupted the conversation. "Pardon me a moment."

"Sure, go ahead," Parker replied. *I have a hunch about some of this, too.*

"What? Where are you going? When you find him call immediately. Do you hear me? And just so you know, Parker is aware of everything now."

"What's up? Where is she?"

"Terri said Frank is gone. He was visiting Loretta when he got a phone call and went into the kitchen to talk. Loretta said the conversation was muffled, but Frank raised his voice several times. A few minutes later, he returned, kissed her, and said goodbye. As he started out the door, the old man hollered, 'Don't forget I loved you first, and *regardless*, I always will ... "

"Regardless of what?" Parker's hand slid to his holster.

Taste of Fire
CHAPTER THIRTY THREE

NO VACANCY blinked in faded pink neon above the Restless Nite Inn. At the end of the single unit row, a Do Not Disturb sign hung on the outside doorknob of room 32.

Newspapers and penciled-in race forms littered the floor of the shabby surroundings.

"Yeah listen, I'm good for it. There's a little dough supposed to come in today, trust me. The next one's a definite. Gotta hunch, I mean tip, so put me down for Bama Broad and Short Cut to Heaven." The phone clicked in Orin's ear. *Crap – hope I'm right.*

He took one last draw off the cigarette and held it between clenched teeth. Stretched out on the rumpled covers of the unmade bed, he allowed the smoke to escape a little at a time. Puff after puff produced almost perfect circles, and he poked at the tiny white zeros in the air. Nicotine stained fingers crushed out the butt in a half-full ashtray. An opaque haze drifted throughout the seedy motel room while a hacking, phlegm-laden cough rattled in his chest. He sat up, spit in the trashcan, and swilled a drink of backwash left in the beer can. A glance at the wind-up clock and anger emerged. The aluminum can crumpled in his grip. *It's late. I expected to hear from Frankie boy by now.*

The drawer of the side table tried to stick as he jerked it open. Some loose change and a lone pack of off-brand cigarettes lay next to the tarnished derringer. "The yellowbelly must be shaking in his boots."

A couple clicks of the remote and a pay-per-view porn movie appeared on the screen of the outdated television. The erotic movements made him restless. Thoughts turned to the brunette and the scuffle at the

TASTE OF FIRE

bar. "Uppity slut. Cross my path again, girlie, and I might have to cash in on a little reimbursement for pain and suffering. I had your ol' mama, and I can have you, too."

Bare feet shuffled to the bathroom. A few minutes later, he flopped down on the dirty sheets, let out a long grunt, and closed his eyes. The jangle of the motel phone made him jump. "Hello? What? Well, it's about damn time."

◆ ◆ ◆ ◆

Shock yielded to rage as Loretta's words seared Frank's heart. Thoughts of vengeance roared like a caged lion. *What a stupid kid I was. How did I ever get mixed up with a beast like Chambers? The jerk ruined my life, defiled the woman I loved and lost, plus denied me a relationship with a child I never knew existed.* Inaudible curses crossed his lips as he sped down the crowded streets of the Alabama town.

A stop at the Short Cut produced a long time friend. One hand on the steering wheel, Frank reached over to hide the pistol with his thin jacket. *Mr. Magnum and me entertained Orin once without incident. This time, we'll finish the job.*

In the driveway of his house, the gears of the old truck grinded as he put it in park. Wrapped in the coat, the gun fit perfect under Frank's arm. The injured knee burned as he limped up the steps to go inside. Thoughts of the task at hand made his heart race like a runaway freight train. Throat dry, he swallowed hard. *Home sweet home, yeah right ... not until I finally fix the mess I caused.*

He sat down on the yellow chenille bedspread and carefully uncovered the gun. A shaky hand positioned it near the pillow. *Dear God, I ain't ever been good at*

195

talking to you much, but I sure need an ear today. Please help me 'cause I know you probably won't forgive me.

The springs of the mattress creaked as he stood. In the bottom drawer of the nightstand, Frank grabbed a small box of ammunition. The pistol rested on the bed, innocent. He picked it back up. The weight of the handle felt cool in his sweaty palm. The click of every shell into the barrel brought renewed strength. *Each one of you babies has a job to do.*

Revenge and resentment fueled the mission. He punched in a number on his cell phone. *It's time.*

◆◆◆◆

"Ah, you want I should leave you at this corner?" The thin, oriental taxi driver pointed.

"Your broken English disgusts the hell outta me." Orin tossed a few dollar bills on the front seat. "Beat it."

A couple blocks from Frank's address, he turned up the collar of the dirty shirt and pulled the bill of a sweat-stained ball cap down lower. Without hesitation, he skulked around landscaped hedges and toward the backside of the designated house. After four quick raps, the door opened slowly.

"Good thing you called, I was about to run out of money," Orin huffed.

Frank winced as the visitor slapped the wounded shoulder and pushed him aside to enter the kitchen. He braced against the hinged door.

"Crap, I'm starving. What cha got to eat?" One hand jerked the refrigerator open.

"How about a slice of this?" Frank replied.

The unwanted guest turned around to meet the .357 pointed square in the center of his chest.

Taste of Fire

"What the …?" In an immediate reaction, both hands flew upward.

"Pull out a chair and sit. Now!"

"Hey, wait a minute, old buddy. Let's not do anything rash here, okay?" A half grin appeared on Orin's face.

"Rash? Not this time, you piece of scum." Steady hands held the weapon as a ray of light from the window glinted off the barrel. "See, I have it all planned out," Frank replied calm and monotone. "Today is the day you *die*." The words rolled pleasantly off his tongue as the back door flew open.

"Frank? Frank? Where are you?" Terri called out. "Your truck is here, but the front door is locked."

The thrust knocked the older man forward. The gun sailed through the air, dropped, and skidded across the crowded kitchen floor.

Frank and Orin scrambled like vipers after frightened prey. Arms and legs flailed and fists pounded. Blood splattered, snot and spit sprayed while chairs tumbled on top of the brawlers.

Terri tried to squeeze around the wooden dinette, but tripped and fell in the middle of the two combaters. "Frank, near the edge of the counter—there it is. Grab the gun!"

As one hand grappled around Terri's neck, Orin scooped up the weapon. The head of the pistol aimed between her breasts. In a breathy pant he said, "We wouldn't want to mess up these big babies, now would we? I got some sweet plans for them later."

Frank lay writhing in pain in the ramshackle mess. The shock of defeat held him immobile, mind languid, and assailed by a terrible sense of bitterness.

Taste of Fire
CHAPTER THIRTY FOUR

Trepidation washed over Terri like a heavy, wet quilt at the reality of the situation. *Why didn't I take Tucker up on his offer to come with me? Dear God, what have I done?* "You, you're the guy at the Short Cut I, I …" She felt the stocky gut of the assailant as one lard arm wrapped around her throat and the other held the gun to the center of her chest.

"Hmm, you smell sweet like a fresh Georgia peach ready to be picked. Yeah baby doll, remember me?" The gun wiggled in his hand. "The name is Orin, but you can call me *Mr. Chambers*. We all got some unfinished business, looks like. Forget any smart ass moves, or I'll finish the job I started on your old bud there."

In single file, Terri in front, the trio walked around the side of the house to the driveway.

Each step shot a chill of fear through her. *Any other time, nosey Miss Fanny would be tending to the Caladiums with the ever-guarding presence of her yappy Schnauzer, Tiger. This is usually about the time Mr. Taylor is delivering the mail. Where is backup when I need it?*

When they reached the yellow sports car, Orin threw an arm around Frank's shoulder. She watched him feign a friendly hug, yet knew the gun, gouged deep into Frank's ribs, belied any camaraderie.

"Drive, you little tramp, and don't try nothin' stupid, or it'll be lights out for the both of ya."

In a cumbersome action, Orin climbed in the cramped back seat of the Mustang. Frank was told to sit up front.

"You gotta be a freakin' monkey to curl up and fit back here." He folded his legs in squaw woman fashion.

"If you don't like it, get out, and go rent a limo." Terri slid in and slammed the door shut.

A large hand slapped the back of her head. "Spunky little witch, but gotta admit, I like a lot of life in my women, makes it more of a challenge. You can't imagine how special this here ride is gonna be."

With the gun positioned between the two front seats pointed at Frank, the kidnapper leaned close to Terri's cheek and licked the side of her face.

The image of a slobbering English bulldog came to mind. Bristles, from the scruff of an unshaven face, felt like nettles, and his breath reeked of decay. A wave of nausea rolled, but she fought to contain any emotion. *Wish I could have introduced this creep to a frying pan during the fracas in the kitchen. Poor Frank. He fought hard to retrieve the gun, but the pain shows. I have to keep a clear head, use my mind. Think, Terri, think!*

"Okay, so where are we going?" The car eased backward.

"Shut up and drive. I'll do the talking. Never did like a woman who jacked her jaws, and damn it to hell if you don't do it all the time," the ogre-like man growled. "Gonna be a memorable night for the three of us."

The tires squealed as Terri ran a stop sign and wheeled around the corner.

Another slap to her head made the car swerve.

"One more wrong move like that girlie, and I swear, I'll blow a hole clean through Frankie boy and your pretty leather seat. It don't make me no never mind."

Taste of Fire

The speedometer slowed in the regulated 45 mph zone.

"Head out north of town. Go past the high school football field and take Parham road until I tell ya otherwise. Got it?"

"Yeah, I got it, but what about gas?" Terri pointed to the fuel gauge. "I only have a quarter of a tank. We probably need to get more. I can just pull into a station and …"

"You think I'm a retard or something? I ain't letting you stop nowhere."

Frank groaned as the gun rammed his side.

"Drive where I said. You ain't gonna need gas when I'm through," Orin hissed.

Natural instinct made Terri want to react to the challenge in his voice, but through the rear view mirror, she could see a glassy haze in his eyes and nostrils flare. The angry retort hardened the features even more as spittle flew with each word.

They drove in silence as wild ideas swirled. Then two blocks up she saw it—a patrol car headed in their direction. *I have to do something quick.* As the black and white passed, Terri honked the horn and flipped the officer off. In an instant, her head jerked back as Orin grabbed a handful of hair, his nasty breath hot on her cheek.

"You stupid bitch," rancor sharpened the tone. "Pull over now, so I can shoot this damn prick," he yelled and moved the gun to the wound in Frank's shoulder.

Frank gasped in pain.

"No, no, please … you don't understand," she pleaded. "It's just a game like slug bug. Whenever the cops see me, I always honk and shoot them the bird. If I hadn't, they would have probably turned around and pulled me over just to give me a hard time. They all know this car. It's only a silly game, I tell you. Ask Frank, he knows. Right, Frank?"

"Yeah, yeah, she's right. Those guys started it years ago. I've told her over and over, it ain't very ladylike, Chambers. She works in a man's world and most of the time acts like one. They jack with her on purpose, so there ain't no choice, but to throw it back at 'em," Frank spoke barely above a whisper.

In the mirror, she watched the thug glance back to see the patrol car turn down a side street.

Taste of Fire
CHAPTER THIRTY FIVE

Patches of silver and blue streaked the late afternoon sky as the Mustang turned off Parnham Road onto a wide gravel drive. Slowly, Terri guided the pale yellow car along as tiny stones pinged underneath and ricocheted off the chassis. Wispy puffs of dust trailed behind the vehicle like tiny storm clouds. She tried to memorize the route in hopes it would aid a later escape.

The knot in her gut pitched as the path ended in front of a vine-covered wooden structure. A twelve-foot chain link fence, rusted from the weather, surrounded the building. A multi-level antenna stood in the distance. The projections gave the impression of a scrawny robot. A continual beacon white light blinked on the top; a warning to low aircraft. Scraggly brush and Kudzu grass outlined the back portion of the opening that blended into a tunnel of trees and dense woods. The seclusion unnerved Terri.

A few years back, she came out to this area when the fire department responded to a house fire farther down the farm-to-market road. The house was still in the rural city limits of the town, but barely. Vast hay pastures and various farmhouses were scattered amid a power line right-of-way. Still, no one close enough to hear a cry for help.

The car slowed to a smooth stop in front of the small building. She left the engine running and reluctantly pushed the gearshift into park.

"Look familiar, chippie?" Orin let out an evil laugh.

"I guess we're somewhere in the boondocks. You tell me," Terri snipped.

TASTE OF FIRE

"It's the boonies all right, baby. I brought your mama here many years ago." He sat back in the seat and chortled louder. "Had myself a rip-roaring good time that night, but nothing ..." He sat up straight, the gun now pointed at Terri's neck. "Nothing like I'm gonna have with you, sugar pie. Yeah, this here was some good ol' stompin' grounds. Hell, right after I got back in town, I grabbed me a whore and a six pack just to check it out again."

Terri could feel the hot, ghastly breath waft around her. She forced back the urge to vomit.

"Now—everyone outta the car," he barked.

Towering oaks formed a canopy over the entrance of the building, shady and obscure where the car sat. A dusty breeze kicked up, and Terri noticed foreboding clouds start to form. *I could run and disappear in the woods before that maniac ever made it out of the back seat. The area is vaguely familiar; help can't be too far away. But ... what about Frank? I can't leave him. Orin would kill him out of spite. Parker, you idiot! Didn't you see me flip you off or hear me honk the horn? Are you blind and deaf? Why didn't you turn around and come after me?* A sense of hopelessness loomed.

Outside the vehicle, thoughts turned to Tucker. *I miss you, need you, and ... I love you. How could I doubt those feelings?* Those navy blue eyes—would she ever see them sparkle again? Would he ever hold her in his arms, make her feel safe or have the opportunity to dissolve into euphoric ecstasy?

"Arggh," Orin groaned. "Damn, I was twisted up like a jacked up pretzel back there." Arms straight over his head, he stretched, the gun pointed toward a deepening indigo sky. Without warning, he spun around toward the lock on the fence and pulled the trigger. Butter yellow sparks skyrocketed as the metal of the small lock ripped back like a peeled banana, and the pieces descended to the ground.

Terri screamed.

Frank's arms locked around her. "Orin, was all that really necessary?"

Lips pursed, he pretended to blow smoke from the pistol like a gunslinger. "You ain't seen nuthin' yet." He lumbered over to the building and placed the nose of the gun against the doorknob. After one blast, the handle was replaced by a bored out hole reminiscent of a belly button. A swift kick from his muddy boot, and the damaged door burst open with the sound of a detonated charge.

"Inside, you two." The tip of the pistol directed the demand.

Terri grabbed Frank's hand, and they entered the dark square room. Huddled together, she whispered in his ear, "I love you."

Four lights split the inky blackness as Orin flipped the switch. Roaches scurried, and a musty odor hung like a thick veil.

A matrix framework of metal supports stood row after row like skeletons on a scaffold. The template pattern of cables and multiple colored tubes veined from one square box to another like a colony of cobwebs invaded by a mass of spiders. Tiny red, amber, and pale green lights blinked from a multiplicity of equipment. Others beeped back and forth in an alien sonorous of communication. A symphony of harmonics chimed euphonically unaccompanied in the vacated seclusion.

In one corner sat a small metal desk with a couple of empty coffee-stained Styrofoam cups stacked on top of one another. The trashcan, filled with beer cans and papers, threatened to spill over to the gritty floor below. Two rows of black manuals sat halfway upright. A cinder block propped against the wall substituted for a bookend on each level. A few chairs and small step stool finished out the inside décor.

Terri scanned the windowless surroundings. "What is this place?"

Orin held the gun in their direction as he stutter stepped toward a large Palmetto bug. "Honey pie, this here is what they call a regen in the telecommunications industry." As his foot found the intended target, a sickening pop announced the successful murder. Nasty remains of the horrid insect splattered on the dirty tile floor. "Got him," he snarled.

"Regen is short for regenerator," Frank added.

"Well, listen to Mr. Wizard over there," Orin spat. "I'll be doing the tellin'. See sweet cheeks, the cable comes in here, rock and rolls around, and gets sent to the next one. It all ends up back at the central office and makes your fancy dancy phone work. Done by the magic of fiber optic cables." He snapped two fingers. "Thing is, this place ain't used any more. It's abandoned 'cause a new one got built on up the road a ways. Everything in here is bypassed. Guess they left it for back up."

"All this technology would appear a bit over your head," Terri quipped.

A purple-pink tongue rolled across yellowed teeth, and an eyebrow rose. "I guess you think I ain't the sharpest tool in the shed, but my daddy use to work for Alabama Telecom. The old fart would drag me out to help his sorry ass. I always hated it, and then one day, it hit me … what a great place to go screw." His head rolled backward in a guffaw.

She shivered as the words echoed in her ears, and a visual of Loretta's ordeal emerged.

In a hip swaying strut, Orin sauntered forward and grabbed her around the waist, the gun still pointed toward Frank.

"You ain't never had what I'm gonna give you. Remember our first meeting at the Short Cut Bar and Grill?" A hand slid to his crotch.

"Orin, shut your mouth," Frank growled.

"Look, she decided to give *me* something I never had, right? Well, now it's only gentlemanly to return the favor." The tip of his nose met hers. "This day's been a long time coming, baby, but hell, I believe it was worth waiting for."

Little by little, he marched her backwards, the gun pointed at Frank, until a metal column slammed against her shoulder blades.

Both hands against his chest, she tried to resist the intrusive embrace. Melded against a blubbery stomach, she closed her eyes and said a silent prayer. Warm slobber trickled down her neck as he taunted more.

In one quick whirl, he turned her to face Frank, hands behind her back.

What is wrong with you Terri Neal? How many self-defense classes have you taken in the course of your career? Get a plan of action together. No one knows where you are, and no one is going to find you, until it's too late.

"Mr. Gunnison is a smart man, cupcake. He ain't gonna try to save ya 'cause he knows he can't even save his own wimpy butt. Ain't that right, you cowardly cuss?" The captor stuffed the gun in the waistband of the worn blue jeans as Frank stood helpless in the middle of the room and watched.

Several inch-wide tie-wraps lay on the floor. Orin quickly devised makeshift handcuffs and bound Terri to the framework, hands over her head.

"Yeah, Frankie boy. You oughta get a kick out of this. Now, sit your old shot up ass down in that chair."

"Look, you don't need to do this, Orin. What's it gonna take to make this right again? You want me to sign over the deed to my club? Think about it—you'd be a real business owner, respected by the community. Let those old skeletons die, and let's mend any bad blood between us."

"Squirm old man, squirm. Ain't nothing gonna fix this until I've had my vengeance from *your* sweet little girl."

"Wh ... what?" Frank choked out the words. "You *knew* Terri was mine all along?"

"Crap, ya'll really are freakin' dumb. Even *I* figured it out way back when." He turned toward Terri. "Your slutty mama played hide the weenie with this lame loser then ran to the open arms of a handsome hunk to save her reputation." He wiped the back of his hand across his mouth. "Shoot, she didn't want the kid ... tried to kill ya by wrecking the car. When that didn't get rid of the unwanted brat, she ran off in the night like a scared raccoon." A cough rattled from his chest, and he spit on the gritty floor.

"Lies! Those are all lies. Don't talk like that," Terri screamed.

A few steps closer and a large hand squeezed her cheeks until she winced. "Now, you ain't in no position to be telling me what I can and can't say. Besides, I'm bored with all this chatter. Time to take care of things, and Frank, you're first."

In a few minutes, Frank sat in the metal desk chair, each hand tie-wrapped to the arms.

"This should give ya a front row view, *Daddy*."

"Orin, don't do this. Please. Okay? I have more money, and we can go get it. Like I said, I'll sign over the deed. We'll go to the bank and get it all done legally. You can either run it or sell it. Hell, you could even burn it down and collect the insurance money. How about that? I would help you do it and keep my trap shut just please rethink this stupid plan," Frank pleaded.

"Stupid plan? Stupid plan?" Orin gritted his teeth. "Let me tell you about the *plan*." The barrel of the gun lodged between Frank's eyes. "First, my reason why. Years back, you thought you was too good to be friends with me after fallin' for that skinny tramp, Loretta. Yeah, I watched her prance that tight caboose around like some high dollar mare and laughed in my face every time I came on to her. No, she wanted *you*. So, I waited. Waited until the time was right—the night you two had a little spat. She was standing outside the gate of the football stadium." Orin paced between Frank and Terri as the reverie flooded out.

"Oh my God." Frank lowered his eyes. "I was supposed to take Loretta home from the game. I thought she was flirting with you, and it made me mad. I told her to … to find her own ride."

"Nope, she wasn't flirting with me," Orin whined like a girl. "She kept saying how much she loved you and wouldn't touch me with a ten foot pole. About the time I walked off, you showed up and started the little lover's quarrel. I slid around behind the athletic building and listened. Had a hard time not letting you hear me laugh my head off, too." He slapped his leg. "You left, like a big dummy, and things played right into my hands. No good Orin Chambers became the white knight and offered the fair lady a ride in his souped up chariot. She was a little skittish at first, but soon hopped in that beat up Pontiac. There was a new bottle of Jack Daniels tucked under the seat, and we came to this magnificent palace to share it." On one foot, he wheeled around, arms in the air. "I stripped off her clothes and poured whiskey all over that thin little body. Man oh man, she kicked and screamed." He smacked his lips. "I licked off every tiny drop of Mr. Daniels before forcing the rest of the bottle down her throat." Meaty hands clapped together. "Being a young buck, I'd never seen a woman so drunk, eyes all rolled back and ripe for the picking. Damn, I took a chance 'cause somebody coulda showed up—had to be quick, but it was worth it, and what a thrill." He took a step toward Terri.

"Leave her alone!" Frank bellowed.

The lights in the regen flickered like a strobe light as a clamorous roll of thunder resonated.

Startled, Terri jerked, unsure which frightened her more, the adverse weather or the reprehensible pursuer.

Orin looked from one hostage to the other. "Woohoo, rain will provide even less chance for anyone to hear your screams of ecstasy, honey." He placed the gun on the small desk. An evil grin appeared as he approached, drool at the corner of his mouth. Rough hands started at the top of her head and slowly caressed her face, shoulders, breasts, and hips. Stubby fingers toyed with her clothes.

TASTE OF FIRE

A hand reached inside his pants pocket, and Terri drew in a breath.

The large pocketknife clicked open in his grip. "How ya like this, my little pretty?" Snorting sounds and moans registered deep in his throat. The edge of the silver blade slipped between the middle buttons of her orange plaid blouse.

Terri closed her eyes, afraid of the next move. *Open your eyes stupid. He wants you to think this is killing you. Play the game!*

Taste of Fire
CHAPTER THIRTY SIX

The folder fell open, and papers scattered in a rush to the floorboard of the patrol car.

"For Pete's sake, be more careful with the evidence, Grimes," Parker chastised the fellow officer.

"Sorry Sarge, but you ripped through the file like a Texas tornado. Tell me what you're looking for, and I'll try to find it." The younger cop gathered the errant documents and grouped them in a semblance of order. "Couldn't we go over this back at the PD in the conference room? I didn't mind bringing the lab reports to you, but its kinda cramped quarters here, and it's getting dark. Not to mention, the light is crappy in your squad car."

"I'm not gonna have a bunch of lurkers asking questions, and time is of the essence. This mall parking lot works fine. Learn to improvise, Corporal." Parker spread the sheets on the dash. An index finger scanned each line. "Okay, here it is. I thought the forensics tech mentioned a type of grass or weed indigenous to the area."

"What?"

"Look, don't you participate in the Hunt and Hike for Health group outings for kids in the County's wayward youth program?"

"Yeah, every other month or so, but what does it have to do with a forensic report?"

"Read this, and tell me where I can find it."

Ray Grimes gripped the heavy-duty flashlight and guided the arc across the paper. "Let's see, last month the organization sponsored their annual arrowhead and rock dig north of town out off a farm-to-market road near Parnham. We blazed a trail through heavy brush to reach a small creek bed running south. The best shot to find anything was a region the locals call Crooked Creek. The Historical Society validated the rock and undergrowth as actual Indian tribal grounds."

"Get to the crux of my question, Grimes."

"Yes sir, seems I remember seeing this type of wild plant growth around there. It's tiny, about a quarter of an inch in diameter, four petal flowers, sorta pinkish, and prickly. Silly things get caught in the knobby pattern of your boots. My wife always makes me take mine off at the front door. It sparked my attention 'cause at one time I wanted to be a botanist. However, since my favorite uncle was a Bama cop, I changed my mind, and decided to …"

"Yeah, yeah, yeah — get back in your patrol car and follow me," Parker interrupted.

"Ten four, Sergeant." Ray saluted.

◆◆◆◆

Terri tried to focus on her feet, the coral-colored Fatbaby boots she wore on the first visit to Skirts and Spurs. They were a stark contrast to the faded beige design of the linoleum floor. A fortified breath filled her lungs. Like a sleeping bear disturbed midway through the winter, adrenalin raced through her veins. Skin prickled at the idea, and a transformation engaged. The hair on the back of her neck stood as she raised her eyes to a full vision of the man who held them hostage. She concentrated on his merciless gaze, obviously hopeful of a pliant surrender. The tip of her tongue crossed her bottom lip.

Orin took the bait and moved in closer.

Clammy palms skimmed her arms, rib cage, and waist. His eyes delivered a message.

Taste of Fire

The next move would be more demanding, daring, devastating—but she was ready. "Stop," she said without a flinch.

The one small word threw him off guard. He blinked, furrowed a brow, and stepped back.

"What the …"

"Look, if you think that doesn't arouse me you must be some sort of lunatic," her voice remained calm.

"Little T?" Frank muttered.

"Oh shut up, Frank. I can't stand any more. Why couldn't I see it before now? This big lug is handsome and hot."

"Yahoo." Orin bent over in laughter. "Maybe you *are* like your old mama after all. She didn't fight me either, course she was drunk as a skunk. Plus, those little pills I popped in the Jack seemed to make it even better." He flipped the knife back into his pocket.

"Do it again Chambers, caress me," she dared. "Better yet, come here and let me do something to you."

After a small step forward, the clumsy man halted. "Oh hell no, I know your pranks. You kicked me once, made me black and blue for a week. Not gonna fall for it again," he huffed.

"Okay … it's true, we got off to a bad start, but I didn't realize what a fireball you are, beefcake. Besides, my hands are bound." Seductively, she flipped her hair back. "Let me whisper what I want." She gave a coquette smile.

Slowly, Orin approached then glanced toward gun on the desk.

"Honey, the stupid gun isn't going anywhere. How could it? Concentrate on me, I need more, big man," she bribed.

Taste of Fire

Frank fought fiercely against the hard plastic on his wrists. As the scene played before him, he lowered his head. "Please, leave Little T alone."

"Poor old goat, you really don't get it, do you? After a stroll down memory lane with your daughter, I'll waste the both of you and leave the remains to rot. By the time anyone finds ya'll, its gonna smell sweet as dead chickens in a boarded up coop.

"Orin, oh Orin, it's me, Lou." *I need to distract him from Frank.*

"Who the hell is Lou?" A quizzical expression formed.

"Lou is a wild woman, the she-devil I become when I get the ache for a real man." The words manipulated an invitation.

Buttons flew in every direction as he ripped off his shirt to reveal a fleshy belly and hairy chest. A worn leather belt zipped through the loops, and in a circular motion, Orin popped it overhead like a bullwhip.

Breath caught in her throat at the image. *Dear God, give me strength.*

The grotesque actions were reaching a fast peak, and Terri needed to act first. "Sweetie, let me out of these stupid plastic thingies, and I'll show you the vamp I really am. My old lady couldn't compare 'cause she didn't appreciate your manly attributes."

Rough, grimy hands grabbed her face, and tobacco-stained lips engulfed her mouth like a vacuum cleaner.

The bile taste made her gag, but she took the challenge and arched away from the metal rail.

"Shit, you taste sweet as sugar." He stumbled backward and paused.

A gritty sound brought a shudder.

Taste of Fire

Orin strutted in burlesque style and inched down the rusty zipper of his jeans.

This is it Terri, this is it. There may not be another chance.

In Zorro fashion, he whipped out the pocketknife and slashed the plastic cables.

As a sign of trust, she left her hands above her head and forced another seductive smile.

The second he leaned forward, her grasp on the metal bar tightened. In one rapid move, both legs wrapped around his waist, feet locked together, and she pushed hard. The motion sent them toppling to the floor, rolling toward the desk like a wayward snowball. In seconds, she flipped him over, but in a flash, the stout aggressor was back on top. Gasps of exhaustion escaped from her throat under the crush of weight.

From inside a bootstrap, he produced the small Derringer. "Oh no, not again." A brutal blow pulverized the right side of her face.

She heard the threat as consciousness faded.

♦♦♦♦

Perspiration dripped from Frank's head. At the sight of the impact, an incredible strength emerged. He planted both feet firm on the floor, chair still attached, and started toward the twosome. A belly laugh brought him to a halt, stationary, bent over in the backbreaking position.

"You look like a giant turtle, ya old fart." Orin hollered and clapped his hands. "Sit your ass down and stay there because the show's just started. After I ravage her knocked-out-cold body, I'm gonna kill both of ya, hear? Although, I gotta admit, it'd be more fun to hear her scream and watch you squall."

"Leave her alone. Kill me if you want, but don't harm her. She's innocent," Frank yelled.

"Innocent? She bruised the family jewels that night at your shoddy bar." He stood and snatched Frank's head back. "You're gonna **watch**."

Curled knuckles to the injured shoulder brought a discharge of vomit from the depth of Frank's stomach. The sour spew plastered the assaulter's face and pudgy bare chest.

"Arggh, you're gonna pay now," he growled.

The soiled tee shirt from the pseudo strip lay nearby. Orin wiped his body and returned to the helpless victim on the floor. A groan gurgled as he squatted down and ripped open the plaid blouse.

"God help me, I said stop!" Frank's sweaty wrists slipped free from the plastic restraints, and the chair thudded. A speedy punch caught Orin square in the left temple catapulting him off Terri and sprawled against the cinder block shelves.

Books, wooden planks, and stones crashed on top of the kidnapper. A stifling cloud of dirt and dust burst through the room.

"Terri, Terri, can you hear me?" Frank coughed and tried to lift the limp body. Blood trickled down the side of her head. *My gun, I have to get my gun.*

Another intimidating rumble of thunder resounded as he turned toward the old desk

"Oh God," Terri moaned.

"It's gonna be okay, Little T. Can you sit up? We gotta get out of here."

As Frank helped her to stand, she screamed, "Watch out."

Heavy hands jerked Frank straight up, and he faced the assailer once more.

TASTE OF FIRE

Glassy-eyed, Orin's attack propelled them into Terri and slammed her against the wall.

The two men wrestled on the grimy floor. Multiple punches sent an array of blood. The utterance of grunts, groans, and curses continued as each struggled for control. A broken piece of cinder block lay nearby, and Orin crushed it on Frank's head. The older man lay still, lifeless as the brawl ended.

Outside, Mother Nature's temperament boiled.

Taste of Fire
CHAPTER THIRTY SEVEN

Words roared in her ears, but Terri couldn't decide if it was real or a dream. *Do I hear thunder and rain? Where is this place? My head hurts so bad I can't think.*

"Finally, I'm gonna get a repeat of your whoring mama." A forceful yank drug her across the floor. The material of the blouse ripped into shreds. The blue jeans were gone next to reveal an almost nude body.

Meaty hands brutally groped her breasts and thighs. The physical weight of Orin's body expelled all the air in her lungs.

"I … I can't breathe … help, help me," the words gurgled in her throat.

An explosion of lightning and thunder caused the dim lighting in the room to flicker again.

Head pounding, eyes blurred, she heard a muffled voice.

Orin halted the unspeakable abuse and pushed to stand up. "**You**?"

Who is it? Amid ear splitting thunder, sounds from the wake of another struggle ensued, then silence. A distinct odor piqued her senses.

I, I know that smell—oh Lord! On hands and knees, she fought to stand. She rubbed her eyes and tried to focus upward. Scarlet and amber flames raced across the ceiling as a billowy black haze barreled down and smothered the room.

"Wake up, honey. There isn't much time," a welcome familiar voice beckoned.

"Daddy?"

Through ebony smog, the face of Chuck Neal smiled.

Smoke filled her nose. She gagged and coughed.

TASTE OF FIRE

Face down on the floor, Orin lay in a large puddle of blood, the back of his head split open—Frank alongside him.

"It's over, sweetheart. You must get to safety and take Frank with you. He's a good man, and you both have my blessing."

An outstretched hand reached to touch the image. "Daddy, I miss you so much."

"This old building is like kindling. Listen to me. You have family and a full life ahead. Hurry, baby-cakes. Get out, now. Don't fret about this scum. He's about to get the taste of fire he deserves."

Half-naked, she tugged on Frank's arm. "Please wake up. We have to get out … the place is on fire, Frank." One hand cupped on top of the other, she started CPR. "Frank!"

A hard cough erupted, and his eyes batted open. "Little T," he whispered.

"Daddy said we have to get out. Come on!"

Frank rose to a sitting position, mouth agape at the nudity. "Oh God, did Orin … I mean, here … take my shirt. Cover yourself."

The couple stumbled through the acrid charcoal mist. Shoulder to shoulder they pushed open the door.

A rush of deathly smoke escaped.

"Help me, help me," a faint cry begged.

Terri turned to see her father's face in the fiery reflection vanish.

Tortured screams echoed while spearheaded flames rotated like a furious tornado and consumed the body of Orin Chambers.

She ran a hand over the scar on her arm and smiled.

◆◆◆◆

Taste of Fire

"Grimes, did you get the call to respond with a fire unit on Parham Road?" Parker checked the microphone.

"Yup, right behind you, Sarge. Good thing we were headed out there anyway."

"Not sure of the information dispatch received—said smoke visible from an undisclosed site. Guess we'll see upon arrival." He flipped on the siren and emergency lights. Dang, it's almost dark. I didn't need another delay in checking out my theory."

"What would that be, Sarge?"

Parker saw the lights of patrol car behind him follow suit. "Tell you later, Ray." *That character at Frank's house, Billy Jones ... it just clicked. The sample of dirt from the crime scene at the Short Cut could be the same I saw embedded in his old boot.* "Central—253, in route, but I need a favor."

◆ ◆ ◆ ◆

Sirens sounded as the fire truck turned on the country road. Gray smoke swelled in the dusky distance. Chief McRae motioned to the rookie driving. "Looks like someone standing by a row of mailboxes up ahead—stop and see what it's about."

The arms of a young woman waved through the beam of headlights. "Ma'am, can we help you?"

"Thank goodness, you're here. Something's on fire up the road. My dog started to howl, and I was afraid there was a prowler, but after I went outside, I smelled it. Hurry! We haven't had much rain lately. Please save our hay pastures."

"Thanks, we'll handle it," the elder firefighter replied.

A quarter mile farther, the unit pulled onto a gravel drive and spotlighted the target.

Taste of Fire

"What in the world? Isn't that Neal's car?"

◆◆◆◆

Gravel flew as the two patrol cars came on the scene.

Sergeant Green ran to the fire chief standing at the back of an ambulance. A woman lay on a gurney, another man stood near.

"What happened? Terri, is that you? And Frank?"

A compress cradled the right side of her face, one eye swollen shut. "Glad you're here, Parker."

"Are you guys okay?"

"I'm fine, just worried about my little girl."

"How you like my new make-up?" She removed the pad to reveal a large swollen contusion and crimson gash.

"Who attacked you? How did the fire start? Why in the world were you and Frank way out here anyway?" A barrage of questions rolled.

"It's my fault we got kidnapped, and I guess lightning caused the fire," Frank replied.

"Kidnapped?" Parker's hand slid to his holster. "Grimes, get over here!"

The young cop appeared in an instant. "Yes sir?"

"Need to get started on this investigation. Take notes, and get some back up."

Ray addressed the situation. "Frank, what can you tell me?"

"First off, this wasn't his fault," Terri interrupted. "Orin Chambers brought us here at gun point. He's the same guy who shot Frank at the Short Cut, isn't that right?"

"Yes, yes. Orin shot me. I lied when I said it was a mugging. I planned to kill him today, but things went haywire."

"Whoa, fella. Watch how you word this," Parker warned. "Do you know the man?"

"Yeah, an old ghost from the past, and you met him at my house ... said he was my cousin, Billy Jones, but it was all lies."

"Actually, I figured that part out. I had Janie at the PD check and see if a Billy Jones bought a ticket at the bus depot. Got the info back a little while ago. So, Billy Jones and Orin Chambers are one in the same?"

"Yup, made me pay him to keep quiet, or he'd hurt the people I care about. After a few things were revealed to me recently, I'd had enough. Called Chambers today and told him to meet me at my house if he wanted another payment. The plan was to make *him* pay. Instead, Terri showed up. Next thing I know, we're in the car and ended up at this old regen." Frank shook his head. "He started ... he tried to do terrible things to Little T. Had me bound in a chair, and she was unconscious on the floor. I managed to get free, and we fought. Guess he knocked me in the head, too. Terri and I barely made it out before the building exploded."

"I, I saw a shadow," Terri spoke up.

"Can you be a little more specific?" Ray paused.

"The smoke was thick, choking, I couldn't tell. Oh God, my head hurts."

"That's enough information, Grimes. Terri, don't try to talk any more. The fire is out, and I'll get with forensics."

"But he, he didn't make it out," Terri whispered.

"Okay Grimes, forward this info to CID, pronto."

"I'm on it, Sarge."

"Get these people loaded up and this ambulance rolling," Chief McRae shouted.

Taste of Fire
CHAPTER THIRTY EIGHT

The presence of woodsy cologne created a rush of sensual memories, and Terri's eyes blinked open. For a second, the vague image at her side produced alarm. As it came into focus, she relaxed. A familiar pair of blue eyes gave a reassuring sense of safety. She touched the puffy area of her face. "Crap this hurts."

"Tsk, tsk, Ms. Firefighter, looks like you'll do just about anything to get my attention." Tucker placed a stethoscope on her chest. "Take a few deep breaths please." A penlight clicked, and for a split second, the bright beam pierced each pupil. "A slight concussion and contusions to the right orbital socket, but other than that, no reason why you can't go home this morning. I'll give you a prescription for some pain meds."

"Frank, where's Frank?" She tried to sit up.

"Hey, settle down. He's fine, just stepped down the hall to visit Gladys and Margie. Who can resist their coffee and bagels, right? After a thorough examination, and a few minor stitches, I kept him overnight. We slept in my office. Neither one of us wanted to be very far from you."

She exhaled slowly. "Tucker, thank you so much. I'm very grateful."

"You are my world, Terri Neal." He took her hand. "Loretta has been worried sick about the two of you. I'm taking the release papers down to the front office. When I come back, we'll get your things, and I'll drive the dynamic duo home."

♦♦♦♦

TASTE OF FIRE

Heavy dew sparkled on the grass as Tucker pulled to the curb. On the front porch of the southern-style cottage, Wade and Weston waved.

"We're sure glad to see you're okay, Sis, Dad," Weston quipped.

Wade opened the screen door. "Come on in. Mom's been a nervous wreck."

As they entered the kitchen, Loretta sat crying softly, one hand wrapped in a wet linen dishtowel.

"Mom?" Terri called.

"Oh, thank God. Terri and Frank!" The older woman jumped up and gave each a hug.

"Hey lady, you're still under my care, too." Tucker replied. "Can't have you getting all excited. By the way, what happened to your hand?" Carefully, he removed the cloth. "Looks like a pretty bad burn, at least second degree. Let me get my black bag. I have some antibiotic ointment to put on those blisters."

Loretta nodded. "Thank you, son."

"We've got more company," Wade announced.

Parker Green spoke to Tucker as they passed in the doorway. "Hello everyone. Sorry to bother you folks at such a time, but we really need to talk."

The group gathered in the living room, and Terri and Frank recanted the details of their nightmarish ordeal.

"And you believe there was another person in there?" Parker scribbled on a small note pad.

"Yes, I heard Orin speak to them. There was a scuffle. The next thing I know, I'm surrounded by flames."

"Chief McRae's official report stated lightning hit one of the communication towers shorting out the old equipment. A live electrical charge shot through the

TASTE OF FIRE

wiring and cables. Because the structure was already deteriorated, it's no surprise it caught on fire in a flash. The outside was overgrown, and any papers or trash acted as a catalyst. It went up like a hot air balloon. Lucky you two got out in time. Can't say the same about that dirt bag, Orin Chambers."

The cop glanced from Terri to Loretta. "See, I had a hunch, so I dug a bit deeper with the forensic team's help. Turns out the idea was right. Pains me to tell you ladies this, but Chambers was responsible for Chuck Neal's death."

Both women gasped.

"How? What do you mean?" Terri's eyes widened.

"I'm sure you heard the same rumors I did, your dad committed suicide and some silly garbage about going down in flames. From the file information, a few weeks prior, Chuck didn't pass the psychological evaluation. I suppose folks assumed the worse. What actually happened was he walked in the hardware store when that scum was in the middle of robbing it. Seems the youngster behind the counter took the first opportunity to flee. Mr. Neal tried to thwart the crime, but the jerk knocked him out. Next, he doused kerosene around everywhere and set the place on fire. My guess, it was an attempt to cover up the foiled plan. He also had presence of mind to lock the front and back doors. I found out he escaped through a small storage window, the only other opening. My boys, and Chuck's fellow firefighters, couldn't get to him in time. The Captain perished, but from smoke inhalation. Maybe it wasn't totally premeditated, but Orin's actions resulted in the loss of a life. Sorry to be the bearer of such bad news, but you needed to know the *real* truth." Parker lowered his eyes.

TASTE OF FIRE

"But the reports said," Terri began.

"The reports were doctored because Orin had an old girlfriend working at City Hall. Don't worry; she's behind bars as we speak."

Smoke inhalation. That explains why I saw his face in the vaporous haze. Eyes closed, she smiled and drew a breath. *Thanks, Dad. I'll always love you.*

❖❖❖

"Thank you, Tucker," Loretta replied.

"No problem. I'll leave some salve samples." His medical bag snapped shut.

"Nasty burn you have there. How'd it happen?" Parker raised an eyebrow.

Fidgety, her eyes darted from the officer to the doctor. "Silly me. Got careless with a hot pot."

"Better let those boys do the cooking for a while, ma'am."

Loretta nodded. "Yes, of course, good idea."

"Well, I have a ton of paperwork to fill out at the PD."

Terri walked over and gave him a big hug. "Thank you, Parker. We owe you a huge debt of gratitude."

Loretta struggled to stand, and Tucker braced her elbow. "Yes, thank you for all the hard work."

The cop put an arm around the older woman's shoulder and gently took the uninjured hand in his.

While everyone chatted, Parker's fingers wrapped around Loretta's.

She felt something slip inside. A glance revealed a slightly scorched half heart pendant.

"Maybe you should be more careful, Miss Loretta." He winked and kissed her cheek. "Well Doc, looks like the *best* man won," he chuckled and looked at Terri.

"What do you mean by that snide remark?" Terri positioned herself between the two men.

"It's nothing, sweetheart. He meant I won the prize."

"Prize? What am I, some sort of damn award to the two of you?" She bolted for the front door, Tucker in pursuit.

The couple continued an animated conversation on the front porch as the rest of the group watched through the screen.

"Come on, baby. The last few days have been rough for all of us. I'll just be glad when we're finally married and things can settle down. You know, when you can spend some time at home. Listen, I have a bottle of your favorite wine, a chardonnay du bois. Want me to go get it?"

Terri stood arms akimbo. "Just what are you getting at? I love you, but I won't be controlled. If you think for one second I'm going to quit *my* job, buster, forget it. In fact, I think I'll go to the Station House right this minute and check in with Chief McRae ... and the guys. For your information, I'm not one of those ditzy women who can be bribed. Come along if you want, but don't get in my way."

Parker started to laugh. "Whew, I might have lost the *prize*, but it seems I may have won after all. Perhaps I should've told the poor guy he'd have his hands full with that little wild cat. Don't mind me, folks, but I think I'm gonna slip out the back door."

Frank cradled Loretta to his side.

They looked at one another then at couple outside and shrugged.

In unison the words spilled out, "She's *your* daughter!"

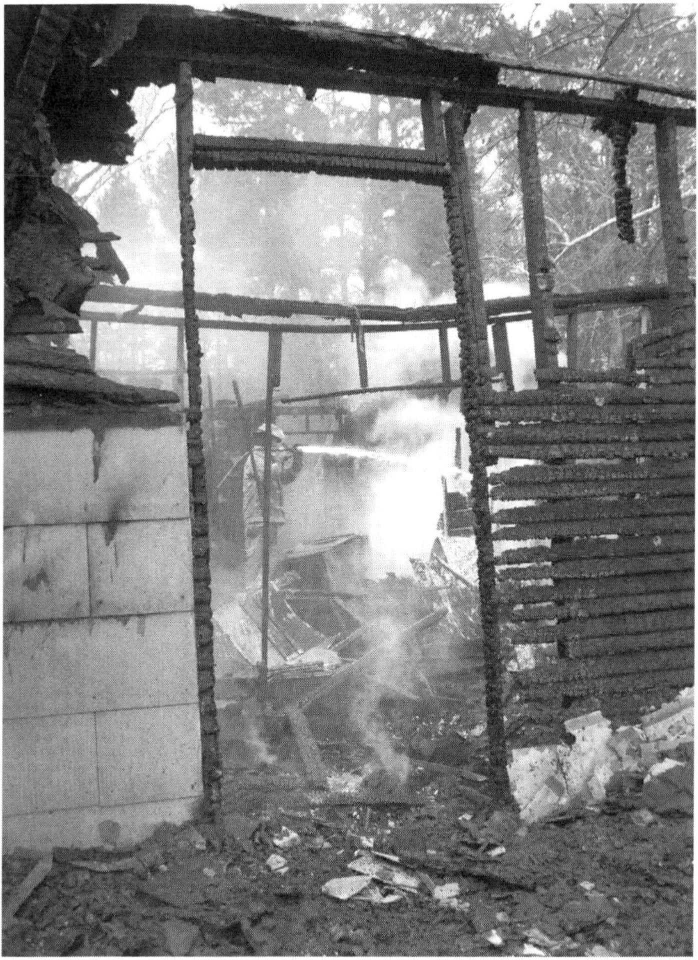